MOON MIRROR

Alathi voiced a sound which was very old, reaching back into the first beginnings of her people, beginnings which even legends could not touch. She took a high step, her eyes only for the moon shape.

Then —

Pain! So sharp that it split through her skull like the blade of an axe. Distant sounds broke through the envelope of the dark.

"—Hill Cat! Best cut her throat, lord. They're as treacherous as a bal-serpent and nearly as deadly. Do they not dance evil down from the moon and spread it abroad in the dark of night?"

"Stand away! This one has in her what I have long sought. If you fear, then back with you. She is indeed a holder of power past your guessing!"

Tor books by Andre Norton

The Crystal Gryphon
Flight in Yiktor
Forerunner
Forerunner: The Second Venture
Gryphon's Eyrie (with A. C. Crispin)
Here Abide Monsters
House of Shadows (with Phyllis Miller)
Imperial Lady (with Susan Shwartz)
Moon Called
Moon Mirror
Ralestone Luck
Wheel of Stars
Wizards' Worlds

THE WITCH WORLD

Tales of the Witch World 1
Tales of the Witch World 2
Four from the Witch World

MAGIC IN ITHKAR (Editor, with Robert Adams)

Magic in Ithkar 1
Magic in Ithkar 2
Magic in Ithkar 3
Magic in Ithkar 4

ANDRE NORTON

MOON MIRROR

TOR
fantasy

A TOM DOHERTY ASSOCIATES BOOK
NEW YORK

MOON MIRROR

Copyright © 1988 by Andre Norton Limited

A TOR Book
Published by Tom Doherty Associates, Inc.
49 West 24 Street
New York, NY 10010

Cover art by Yvonne Gilbert

ISBN: 0-812-50303-1   Can. ISBN: 0-812-50304-X

Library of Congress Catalog Card Number: 88-20136

First edition: December 1988
First mass market edition: November 1989

Printed in the United States of America

0 9 8 7 6 5 4 3 2 1

Contents

HOW MANY MILES
TO BABYLON?

"How many miles to Babylon?
Three score and ten.
Can I get there by candlelight?
Yes, and back again."

Sue Patterson shut her eyes and wished she could close her ears as well. The throb in her head which had been only a warning ache this morning, was building into one of the bad times. But if she begged off from this promised hour at the nursery school that would mean explanations. And at the very thought of explanations her fear came, keener and worse than the pain. She could not tell—not unless she had a chance to see J.J. first—and she had not seen or talked to him all week.

She rested her head against the post of the tall playground fence, that sing-song coursing through her as if the words were blows. Who ever thought it would be clever to teach the kids those stupid songs? Well, she need only look in the mirror. But the Sue Patterson of a week ago was a different person. Looking back now she was dully surprised that she had ever been that person. Then all that mattered was getting through the day so she could see J.J. in the evening.

Well, she still wanted to see J.J. But for a different reason— Her head, it was much worse this morning. And if Bobby Kinney did not stop that screaming—! Her hand clenched at her mouth and she bit hard on her knuckles to choke down a cry of her own. This was the worst time yet. What if— if she could not stand it any longer, let out a scream louder than Bobby's, maybe fell over out here on the playground? What if there was something wrong in her skull ever since—

No! She would not let herself think that! If she let any one know, any one at all, they would start asking questions. And they would get it all out of her, she knew they would—about J.J. and the bike, and—the rest of it!

But where was J.J.? She had called his house twice, and the last time she had to hang up fast when his mother answered.

If her head would only stop hurting so!

There was the bell, Miss Manning was calling in the kids for their milk and crackers and morning rest. Rest—if she could only bundle up somewhere herself.

Sue stumbled away from the fence, began feebly to help Eva round up the children, start them back to the house.

"Say, Sue, you don't look so good." Eva was staring at her. "You feel sick—virus maybe?"

Why had she not thought of that? Of course, they would not want her around with the virus. And she could even use that excuse with Mom. She was sure stupid today.

"I—I guess so. I better tell Miss Manning and go home."

"Right. You know how she is about being sick around the kids."

Leaving Eva to struggle with the round-up, Sue managed to reach the door and Miss Manning. There was no need to put on an act, she must already look half dead, because Miss Manning was staring at her intently.

"Sue, what's the matter? Are you ill?" She spoke sharply but Sue could not blame her. Spread virus here and Miss Manning would find herself with an empty school.

"I'm going home. Guess I have the virus—"

"You had better see Miss Luce at once!"

Not the visiting nurse! Sue swallowed, she felt so sick at her stomach now. And she was stupid again, she had forgotten all about it being Miss Luce's day here.

"I can manage, Miss Manning. Really I can—" She summoned all that was left of her strength and tried to look as if this was no worse than the sniffles.

Miss Manning regarded her doubtfully. But Sue knew she really only wanted to get her away before she spread any germs—or whatever made virus.

"Are you sure you can get home all right, Sue?"

Home? Home was the last place she wanted to go—with Mom there ready to start fussing.

"Sure—I can get home all right." She held on with determination, fighting the sickness which spread from that throb right behind her eyes downward, to dry her mouth, bringing waves of nausea. Maybe she did have the virus. It must be that—it had to!

Sue could not remember much of how she got away from the school. She must have looked and talked all right because Miss Manning let her go, and Miss Manning was nosey.

But she was free, walking down the street. Only in her head that silly rhyme kept repeating over and over:

> "How many miles to Babylon?
> Three score and ten."

What was Babylon? She had a faint idea it was a city—somewhere. Three score and ten—how many did that make? Oh, her head! Twice she leaned against a tree to wait out the waves of pain which blotted out everything but the agony they brought.

She was in the park without knowing how she got there. Sitting on the grass at the foot of a big tree. And she had been sick, there was a nasty mess on the ground. But her head did not hurt so much and she was weakly thankful for that.

If she only knew where J.J. was! She could not remember much of the accident now. It was a violent ending to the peaceful life of a while ago. They had been down at Benny's, playing the juke box and drinking Cokes.

Cokes! Sue shuddered and her stomach heaved. She never wanted to see a Coke, smell one, even be near one. Never, never, never!

Even though she closed her eyes and tried to close out memory she could see a clear picture, a picture of J.J. dropping that pill into his Coke, one into hers, too. Only she had managed to spill it. And that had made him so mad he said he was taking her right home. Sue was afraid of him then but she hated to make a big fuss—

The picture in her mind changed, they were on their way back to town. She could see J.J., his hair sticking out below the edge of his helmet in a rough fringe, feel the wind whipping her own face. And then—

There had been the dog in the road and—and J.J. did not swerve to avoid it at all. He had deliberately run straight at it—laughing! She had screamed. And he had— She could not remember. When she did, she had been lying with her head against the fence post. And when she sat up, feeling so queer, J.J., the Honda, they were gone. Everything was gone but that black thing in the road. She could not make herself crawl over to it, she had gotten away as fast as she could.

Then—there was more she could not remember. Mom and Dad, they had been at the Cape for the weekend, Aunt Martha staying at the house. She had gone to the movie with Mrs. Marland. That was one piece of luck. Sue had been able to get home and into bed. It was like something sort of took over inside her, telling her what to do.

The next morning—J.J. never called. She waited and waited. Why did he act like this? If she could see him, talk to him—

Sue's head sank forward on her knees. She felt so weak, so tired, and it was hard to think. J.J.—he had always been so quiet, and kind, not wild like some of the boys. That's why she liked him, she'd always felt safe—up until Saturday night. If she talked, they might arrest J.J.—with the new laws about drugs and all—they could shut him up for years and years. Maybe J.J. had only been trying out those pills—somebody dared him—something like that. She just couldn't think very straight anymore.

At least her head did not hurt as bad as it had. First she was only dimly aware of that. But she had no desire to get up, go home, go anywhere. Just sit here and—

No pain at all now, only a kind of tingling—not in her head but at the base of her spine. Now that was climbing up along her back. She did not care—the pain was gone. Now it had settled at the nape of her neck. She wanted to raise her hands to the source of that feeling, but did not seem to have enough energy left.

It was in her head now, seeming to push away the memory of the pain. She had no desire to move, instead Sue was aware of an odd feeling that what was *she*, herself, Sue Patterson, was not really a body at all, but something which lived inside a frame of flesh and bones, made that operate by her orders.

The tingling was now behind her eyes where the pain had been the worst of all. But she was not hurting now, she was—

She was afraid! But in spite of that fear there was something else, a need to know, to understand what was happening—that was growing stronger than the fear. She—

No!

Sue could have cried out in sheer terror, yet this other self who lived in the body would not let her. For a terrifying moment or two out of time she—she had not been in that body at all! She had been—above it! She had looked down at Sue Patterson slumped on the ground. Dying—was she dying? No!

Then—she was back. She was safe in her body again. But the pain in her head was still gone, as was the tingling now. All she felt was very weak and tired as if she *had* been sick with the virus.

Had she imagined what had happened? But it was so vivid that she shivered, chilled. Somehow she got to her feet, started home. If Mom asked what was the matter—she *was* sick. Just to get home—safely home!

Mom's car was gone. Sue wavered around the side of the house and fumbled under the loose brick for the back door key. The house was cool, dark after the bright blaze of the sun. She stood in the kitchen, steadying herself with a hand against the fridge. Then she lurched to the sink, let the water run cold before she filled a glass and gulped thirstily. This was real. She was drinking water, was in the kitchen at home. This was real—that other—it had not happened! Of course not! She would go to bed, maybe take a couple of aspirin—

No! The flash of memory of J.J.'s hand poised above the glass about to drop that pill into the Coke was a picture which no amount of time might erase. She filled the glass again and drank feverishly, looking over its rim about the kitchen, to impress the real upon her mind.

There was the sound of a car pulling into the drive— voices— Mom was coming back and someone with her. Sue wanted to escape, but she was too late. Mom and Mrs. Chambers came in carrying overflowing cartons of what looked like a lot of junk—the stuff for the P.T.A. rummage sale.

"Sue! What are you doing home!" Mom dropped her carton on the floor.

There was nothing to do but tell the part of the truth that she dared.

"I got sick—something I ate, I guess. I feel a lot better now—" And that *was* the truth. All the pain which had been with her since the accident and which had swelled at times to that agony such as she had experienced earlier this morning was gone. She just felt tired and weak, but not sick anymore.

"Well." Mom looked at her closely. "You don't look good. You get yourself to bed, young lady. I'll take your temperature. If you hadn't had all those flu shots, I'd think you had the virus."

Mom would fuss, and ordinarily that would have driven Sue wild. But now she did not care. It was good to go to her room, undress and crawl between the covers. But she did not take the aspirin Mom brought. And somehow she was not in the least suprised to learn that her temperature was normal.

Sue slept after Mom left, and it must have been noon when she awoke, with a queer feeling that she had been somewhere else and had done something important, if she could only remember. As she lay there, trying hard to recall her dream, the tingling began again.

She shut her eyes on the familiar walls with their posters, on real life, and felt that sensation once more creep up her body, into her head. But she would not—look!

NO! She was not going to see *that* again. Determinedly Sue fought. And, after what seemed a long time, the tingling was gone, she dared to look about. She was safely in bed, in her body—and this was her room. Also she felt better—hungry—

It must be long after lunch. Sue pulled out of bed, reached for her robe. No headache anymore. She padded along the hall to the kitchen.

The cartons were still beside the table. Mom was gone—maybe for another load. Sue poured a glass of milk, spread a piece of bread liberally with Mom's special raspberry jam and sat down to eat.

She was on her second slice when Jerry banged in, heading

for the fridge. His team cap stuck to the back of his head and he had the beginning flush of a sunburn across his nose. He shed his catcher's mitt on the chair beside her as he passed, kicked at the cartons.

"Thought you were sick," he commented. "Hey, where's that piece of pie we had left over? Did you know Mrs. Mason called—she wanted to talk to you. Mom said you were sick—sleeping—she went in to look."

Sue stopped chewing. J.J.'s mother calling her— She knew again that cold fear she had lived with during the past few days. They would ask questions—

Jerry, with a Coke bottle in one hand, the missing pie in the other, nudged the fridge door shut with his shoulder as he turned.

"Mom's crowd is sure getting in the junk for the sale," he commented as he rounded the cartons to sit down opposite to her. "Say, you don't look too good—"

For a pesty brother, Jerry was not too bad. Sue wished she was as young as Jerry, even as she had been before last Saturday. She put down the rest of the bread and jam slice. Right now she did not feel any better than Jerry thought she looked.

"That Ken, he's a dope. He's got this idea he's a pitcher!" Jerry snorted in disgust, cramming in an out-sized bite of pie and chewing with a vigor totally unrelated to any acceptable table manners. "He can't send one over the plate in ten tries—at least ten tries! The guy's a disaster, a plain disaster, and we've got to live with him." He scowled.

This was real, the kitchen, Jerry, all of it real. Sue had to hold on to that reality. If they asked her about J.J., she drew a long breath—she might have to tell them, except about the pill. But why had not J.J. called?

"What a lot of junk," Jerry repeated, staring down at the carton by his knee. "Who'd want to buy any of this stuff?"

He reached down to pull at the jumble of contents, coming up with a small, brad-studded harness, red in color. Something only a very small dog could wear. It still had a leash attached.

Jerry dangled it up and down by the leash. "Here, Spot!" He trailed it along as if there was a dog in tow.

A dog in tow— Sue blinked. Had she for a moment, a single frightening moment, seen a cream and brown body within that harness? Of course not! Unsteadily she put her hands to her head, closed her eyes, and then looked again. Jerry still held the leash, and the empty harness was lying on the floor. Suddenly she grabbed at it, she had to *know* there was nothing else there.

Her hands closed upon the strips of metal-studded leather, crumpling them together.

But—

It was like the time in the park. Only this time there was no warning tingle, no slow rise of sensation to her head. Instead she saw a picture in her mind.

Sue gave a gasp, dropped the harness.

"Su-Ki! The car hit her—Su-Ki!"

There was no kitchen, but a street, and in the gutter a Siamese cat kicked spasmodically.

"Sue!" Jerry pulling at her arm. "Sue—what's the matter? Who's Suky? Sue!"

She threw the harness from her and the picture was gone. But it remained so vividly in her memory that she could not rid herself of it so easily.

"Su-Ki—she was a cat. She wore that—a car hit her—" she repeated as if she must keep in mind what she had seen, that it was important.

Dimly she was aware of Jerry staring at her as she pushed back from the table, heading for her room. Once in that refuge Sue slammed the door behind her. Shaking, cold with fear, she fell rather than sat on the edge of the bed.

Was this the way people went crazy? She—she had been hit on the head when she fell off the Honda. Then all those headaches— And in the park when she thought she was outside her body— Just now seeing Su-Ki . . . *NO!* She did not know any Su-Ki—she had never seen a cat die. She could not be remembering—it was— She must be going crazy!

Sue bit down hard on the edge of the hand she had raised to her mouth. She could feel the pain of that. This was her own room, she was here—

"Sue!" Jerry pounded on the door, called through it.

"Just let me alone! Let me alone!" her voice was close to a scream.

She had to think, to know— How did a person go crazy? They saw things that were not there— They— She wanted to dive into bed and pull up the covers, bury herself so and never come out. A doctor—suppose she went to Dr. Wilson and told him, and then they took her away to be shut up somewhere— And—

Sue wanted to scream, but she would not let herself. Mom, Dad, Jerry—if she was going crazy—she could— could *hurt* them maybe. Get away—away from here before she did something to someone. Get away where nobody knew her—

She began to dress. Now that she had made her decision it seemed to steady her. She could think, plan a little. She had her allowance for next week. Dad had given it to her this morning. And she had the money she had been saving up to go to the Cape with the Service Club. There was her piggy bank, too—she put dimes in that all year long for Christmas. As she buckled her sandals she counted up her resources.

Then she got out her big purse and put it all in, the wallet with her allowance, the envelope of the club money, last of all the weight of dimes from the piggy bank, not stopping to count. Jerry had gone away. But he would tell Mom—

Sue went to the south window. She could get out here, cut across the yard into the Fentons' drive. She did not know the bus schedule. But if there was not one leaving soon maybe she could hitch a ride. Dad said no hitching ever, but house rules did not count now.

The need to move fast made her stronger. Sue pushed out the window screen, scrambled through, and was down the Fentons' drive and into the back street in no time at all. The bus station was on Vandosia, she could cut over by the library, avoid going down De Sota.

Holding her heavy purse against her Sue stumbled on. She had hurried so fast she was getting a pain in her side and she felt a little dizzy. Better slow up, she did not want to faint or something and fall down right on the street. Maybe she should sit down awhile. The library was closed today, she could sit on the steps at the side where the bushes were.

"Sue! Sue Patterson!"

The name was called so demandingly that it reached even through the fog of fear. She looked up dazedly.

Miss Carmichael stood on the steps, she must have been working alone today. She did sometimes when she got behind. Sue, ready to cry with frustration and fear, found she could not run as she longed to.

"Sue, this is luck, running into you today. There has to be a change in our plans for the Cape. We can't get the bus until—Sue! What is the matter, dear?"

There she stood, wearing one of her book-colored dresses which always seemed to fit in with the shelves and the volumes which were her usual background, her gray hair cut short in ragged little points about her face, looking at Sue like Mom did just before she began to fuss. Sue felt as if she were backed against a wall with no hope of escape. For the first time she thought she could easily hate Miss Carmichael.

"Leave me alone! Just—leave me alone!" Sue flailed out with one arm as if to beat off an expected attack.

"Sue, there must be something very wrong. You need help."

"Just—leave me alone." But Sue could not fight any longer, she felt so weak, so full of fear.

"Sue, come on in the library. You—you are ill."

Sue was hardly aware of the words. In spite of herself she responded to the grasp on her arm which took her away from the walk into the dusky quiet of the big building closed for the weekend.

"Sit here. I will get you some water—"

Sue sat. She was in Miss Carmichael's office. It was stuffy with the smell she always associated with books. The library had always been an important part of her life since she had been old enough for Mom to bring her to pre-school story hour.

It was so quiet and then came the soft whirr of a fan. Miss Carmichael must have turned that on. Sue tried to think. She had to get away, only she was so sick she felt as if she could not stand up.

"Drink this, dear." Miss Carmichael was back with a paper cup of water. Sue drank. She must get up, go— There was the bus—only now the walk to the station loomed in her mind as an endless journey.

Miss Carmichael sat down in her own chair behind the desk which was so covered with piles of papers, books and magazines that these formed a wall between them. Only Miss Carmichael's direct gaze, her obvious concern breached that wall.

"Can you talk about it, Sue?" She was not demanding an explanation, she was offering to listen. Sue understood that. But if Sue told her the truth—how quickly would Miss Carmichael change?

Words choked her, she felt so under pressure she had to talk. Well, why not say the truth? Learn right now what would happen to her when she told?

"I'm—I'm going crazy!" She blurted it out.

However there was no change in Miss Carmichael's expression. She did not look afraid, or lose that concern which reached Sue.

"Why do you think so, Sue?" Her composure had a calming effect. Sue straightened a little.

"Because—" Then, as if she could no longer contain her fear and misery, it all spilled out. The accident, the headaches, that terrible time in the park, and what she had seen when she picked up the harness.

"It's all wrong," she almost wailed. "I never saw a cat die that way, I don't even know anyone who has a Siamese! So you see—I must be going crazy. And I've got to get away. Crazy people do terrible things. I might even—even try to hurt Jerry, or Mom, or Dad—"

"Sue," Miss Carmichael's saying her name in that tone was like a quieting hand laid upon her lips. "Listen to me. You are not in the least insane."

"But the cat—and being out of my body—and—"

"Listen to me carefully, Sue. Have you ever heard of psychometry?"

"You mean—like sending me to a psychologist? See, you do think I am crazy!"

"Not at all, my dear. Now try to use that good brain you do have and listen to me instead of your own fears. Over the past years men have begun to realize that there are indeed talents which can not be measured by the usual standards— paranormal gifts. Psychometry is one of these. Sometimes people are born with such talents. At other times these suddenly develop as the result of illness or injury. It is very true that we use only a small portion of our brains, as if sections are closed off from our control. Illness or injury apparently can break down the barriers between these closed sections. Can you understand me?"

Sue stared at her. "You mean—because I was hit on the head and then had all those headaches—that opened some part of my mind which didn't work before? But why me?"

For the first time Miss Carmichael smiled. "I imagine that particular question has been asked a good many times, Sue. And there is no answer one can give. But now I want you to know this—neither experience you have had (and that those were very frightening for you I can well understand) is unknown. The sensation of being out of the body, able to look down on one's self has been reported many times. And psychometry—the 'reading' of the past history of an object —is relatively common. What you must do is understand fully what has happened to you and learn how to use and control your talent."

"But—how can I be sure—?"

"There are ways of making sure. For the moment you can take refuge in this thought—you are not alone, there are others with the same abilities. Now," she opened the desk drawer, took out a booklet, and flipped over its pages. "There are tests for such talents. You must remember, Sue, that those who develop these gifts are not to use them foolishly, and, if they are not taught how to control them, they face many dangers. There are now foundations set up to study sensitives."

"But—but people think that mind reading and all that stuff is just faking," Sue protested. "They will still say I'm crazy."

"If you talk about it with those wrongly educated, or ignorant, you may have that response, yes. But the first thing you must accept, Sue, is silence on your part, until you have the type of help you need to accustom you to this. Can you keep quiet?"

Sue licked her lips. "What about Mom, Dad, and Jerry? I could keep quiet with other people, but I don't know about them. Jerry knows already there is something wrong by the way I acted in the kitchen."

"Yes," Miss Carmichael had been running a finger tip down the page of the booklet, now she paused. "I can see your problem, Sue. I don't know how much your parents may be ready to accept this. That is why we may bring in an expert in the field—Dr. Muriel Evans."

"A psychologist?" Sue flinched.

"A parapsychologist, Sue. She is the head of a research

department at Stafford. I have met her once; she gave a lecture here at the library three months ago. I shall get in touch with her."

"But—until then?"

"I can not say more, Sue, than to keep as quiet as you can. Do not experiment nor discuss the matter—just be assured that you are not losing your sanity." Miss Carmichael paused. "There is something else, Sue. Now you are frightened, disturbed, as is only natural. But that feeling of strangeness will go. And—this is very important, my dear—do not allow yourself to misuse what has been given you."

"Misuse?" Sue wanted nothing but to be rid of what Miss Carmichael seemed to think was a gift, but what she hated and feared.

"Misuse, yes. You—" Again Miss Carmichael hesitated. "Perhaps the simplest way I can warn you, Sue, is to say that such talents lay a heavy burden on those who possess them. Any advantage which comes from their use must be for the good of others, not for the selfish gain of one who has the gift. Think of that if you are tempted to put your 'seeing' to any test. Say to yourself, Sue, is this for real benefit?"

"I won't use it at all!" Sue returned quickly.

"You think that now. But conditions have a way of changing. Just think before you do, that is important."

Sue gave a sigh. Perhaps it made sense to Miss Carmichael but—

Miss Carmichael stood up. "There have been books written about this, Sue. You haven't been a very steady patron of ours of late but your card is still in force. Suppose you read a little about other people who have had to learn to live with paranormal gifts."

Books—Sue caught at that. "Oh, yes—" she was eager.

But as she neared home, the money-heavy purse against her hip and the two volumes Miss Carmichael had chosen for her under her arm, she began to feel apprehensive again. If Jerry had told Mom about what had happened— Well, she could say she was sick again. If Mom had not yet gone to her room, found that screen out— She had better hurry!

The screen was still loose. Maybe that meant her absence had not been discovered. Sue jerked it farther out, scrambled in and pulled it back into place. The books—she'd put them here in the case. And—

She had just dropped her purse on the tumbled bed when there came a knock at the door.

"Sue! Sue—are you ill? Sue!"

Mom! Sue straightened, to face her reflection in the mirror. She did not look any different. Was Miss Carmichael right about what had happened to her? But there was no reason for the librarian to lie, and she had even called Dr. Evans, made an appointment for Sue to meet with her in Miss Carmichael's house next Saturday. She would not have done that if she had just made up a story to keep Sue quiet.

"Sue!"

"Coming!" This would be the first test, seeing Mom, keeping quiet.

She opened the door. Mom was worried all right. Jerry hovered behind her, his face unusually sober.

"Sue, Jerry said you were—"

"Acting queerly?" Somehow Sue found the words. "I— well, Mom, I was awfully sick. I had to get to the bathroom."

"But this about a cat being killed—"

"It was the harness, Mom. It made me remember something I saw, made me sick."

"Miss Williams gave us that," Mom said slowly. "Her cat that was killed last year wore it. But that was before she moved here. You could not have seen that happen, Sue."

"No—I saw another cat." Sue shivered, and she did not have to act that, remembering only too well what she had seen in that flash of what Miss Carmichael called psychometry.

"I see." But was Mom satisfied? "Sue, if you are ill I want you to get back into bed. And I am going to phone Dr. Wilson."

"What about Mrs. Mason, Mom?" Jerry interrupted. "She said she was coming right over."

"Mrs. Mason?" Sue faltered. Almost during the past hour she had been able to push J.J. to the far back of her mind. Why did his mother want to see her?

"She is quite upset. She seems to think you know something important about James."

Mom was watching her closely. Something about J.J.? Did

his mother know about the pill and want her to be a witness or something? Where was J.J.? All her early worries flooded back. Sue sat down on the edge of her bed.

"I haven't seen J.J. since Saturday. I don't know anything—"

"Sue," Mom was standing right over her now, but she looked over her shoulder at Jerry. "You run along, young man, this is none of your concern."

Sue cringed. Could she face Mom's questions? Could you tell just bits and pieces of the truth and make it sound as if it were the whole story?

Jerry closed the door unwillingly, Mom waiting until he had.

"Now, Sue," she swung back, "just what is going on?"

"I don't know, honest, Mom. I haven't seen J.J. since Saturday."

"Saturday," Mom repeated slowly. "And what happened on Saturday, Sue? You've not been yourself all week. Did you think we didn't notice?"

"I was—sick—"

"Perhaps. And perhaps that sickness has a cause. What happened Saturday night? I want the truth, Sue."

"I—J.J. and I had a fight—then we started home on the Honda. J.J.—he hit a dog in the road. I fell off the bike and, Mom, honestly I don't know what happened then for a while. J.J.—he was just—gone—"

"Sue!" Mom's hands were on her shoulders. "You were

thrown off that machine! You were hurt and never said anything? Child, how could you be so dangerously foolish? I'll run you right over to the clinic now—phone Dr. Wilson to meet us there—"

"No! Please, Mom—I'm not hurt—you can see—"

"I can see nothing. But Dr. Wilson is going to see and you are going to have a complete checkup, X-rays if necessary. Oh, Sue, how could you not tell us about this? The consequences may be serious!"

Sue subsided numbly. There was no arguing with Mom now, she knew that. But if she did not tell the rest—the paranormal thing—they surely could not learn about it with X-rays and stuff. The tests Miss Carmichael had talked about were a lot different. She just had to keep quiet about that.

"No wonder Mrs. Mason wants to see you!" Mom came back from the telephone, indignation in her voice. "If you were hurt because of that machine of James's, it's partly his responsibility. Now come on, Sue, we'll go to the clinic. Dr. Wilson is going to meet us there, luckily I was able to catch him."

"You're a very lucky young lady," she heard some time later. "Bruises, a slight concussion, nothing worse. But you'd better stay off Hondas for a while."

Sue drew a breath of relief. Dr. Wilson had poked and prodded and asked a lot of questions, ordered two X-rays. But he certainly did not ask the questions she could not answer. And Mom was relieved. So relieved that when they started back home she was sharp, talking about new rules about dates, which Sue only half listened to.

There was the Mason car in front of the house. It could be that Mom's guess was right, that J.J. had told about the spill and Mrs. Mason wanted to know if she were hurt.

Still there was something— Sue stirred restlessly, plucking at the clasp of her seat belt as they drove into the driveway. She was uneasy, as if she were sure trouble lay ahead.

Jerry lay in wait at the back door. "Mom—Mrs. Mason —she's—she's awfully queer. She's been crying and she said she just *had* to see Sue."

"She'll see her all right," Mom snapped. "She'll understand how lucky they are that Sue is not in a hospital because of that son of theirs! Come on, Sue."

Mrs. Mason stood by the big front window looking out, but when they entered she turned quickly.

"Susan," her eyes were all puffed and red, "Susan, where is James?"

Startled, Sue blurted out the only answer she knew. "I don't know—"

"When he left Sunday, it was very early, we thought he had gone up to the lake with Ralph Pinner, he'd talked about that. But Ralph came home last night and said James was never there. I—I went through his room—he took his camp money, and I found this lying on his desk!"

She thrust a twisted piece of paper at Sue, who smoothed it out to read:

"No use looking for me, I'm no good. I killed Sue.
First the dog, then Sue. You'll find her on the woods
road near Benny's."

"What," Mrs. Mason's voice scaled up as if she were so
scared she was about to scream, "what does he mean? He
talks about killing you. Is he—is he out of his mind? And
where is he?"

"He—there was an accident when we were coming
home," Sue answered slowly. "J.J. hit a dog in the road—
and I got thrown off the bike. He must have thought I got
killed. When I knew where I was—he was gone—"

"But—but this is totally unlike J.J." Mrs. Mason stared
about her as if she could not understand anything any more.
"J.J. is an excellent rider, he's never had an accident. And if
you fell off—why in the world didn't he stay and help you? I
don't understand this—any of it, Susan. Are you sure that is
what happened? It doesn't sound like James at all!"

J.J., the pill in the Coke. Sue bit her lip. No, it was not like
the usual J.J.

"And where is he now? Do you have any idea where he
might have gone, Susan?"

She was all ready to deny that—but—it was happening
again, the tingling, the awareness. She wanted to run from
their eyes. Mrs. Mason was staring at her so oddly, did she
guess? But surely no one could unless she told. Was—this—
could this psychometry thing tell them anything about J.J.?
And if it did, did she have any right to keep quiet, to deny it?

What had Miss Carmichael said? That it must be used to help others, not herself. This was a test—of the helping part. But if she told what she saw and they asked her how she knew—? And she had no time to think about it either. Mrs. Mason was watching her as if she guessed Sue knew something. She would never believe it now if Sue said no.

"Let me think." Maybe she could fake it, tell whatever she learned by holding this letter so Mrs. Mason would think she was remembering what J.J. might have told her. She closed her eyes—there *was* a picture forming.

J.J.—yes—though he was blurred and she could not see him too clearly. Trees, and some rocks—and water—like the shore of the lake. But Mrs. Mason said he had not been with Ralph. But that did not mean he could not be at the lake—hiding— Because that was what she felt—fear—the need to hide—

"There's—" Sue opened her eyes, ran tongue tip across her lips, gathering her courage, "there's a place up at the lake where there are two big rocks, and some pines, right down by the water—"

"The cove!" Mrs. Mason broke in. "Yes, I know it. And James liked to go there. But how do you know he's there? It's as if you saw him—"

Sue flinched from that guess, hoping that no one would believe that. "He talked about it once—that he liked to go there," she improvised. "That's the only place I know of where he might be—"

"When Ralph came home alone I never thought of James being up there by himself. But it is a place to start looking. Oh, Susan—thank you!"

Before Mom could get a word out Mrs. Mason was on her way.

"Well!" Mom exploded. "When she gets that young man back to town your father and I will have something to say to him. Now, Sue, you go and lie down. Dr. Wilson said no undue strain until he's entirely sure about that concussion. And I am not at all satisfied about this accident story either, young lady—why James went running off that way. There is something very queer about it all."

Sue relaxed, she had gained time, time to think things out. Mom got her into bed and then, mercifully, left her alone. She lay looking at the ceiling, not in the least inclined to sleep as Mom had practically ordered her to. There was such a lot to think about.

How many miles to Babylon? That silly little rhyme flashed into her mind again.

> How many miles to Babylon?
> Three score and ten.
> Can I get there by candlelight?
> Yes, and back again.

Babylon was a city, she remembered that now—a long way off. But she had traveled a lot of miles this afternoon when she had seen the lake and J.J. by it. If Mrs. Mason did find him there—then— It was still frightening, but exciting, too. Things to do, places she could travel to—all hers if she could learn how to do this. Sue smiled slowly; it was the learning which mattered now and that she was going to do, surely and certainly.

THE TOYMAKER'S SNUFFBOX

O nce upon a time when the world of magic was much closer to our world than it is today, there lived in the city of Kammerstadt a toymaker who had his shop at the very end of the Street of Carpenters. So perfect were the toys he made and so well had he learned his trade, that all the kingdom found their way to that shop to buy. No child's Christmas or birthday was complete unless among the gifts was a doll or a box of soldiers, a talking bear or a galloping horse made by Master Franz.

It was often Master Franz's custom to work late in his shop to finish some toy. And one night while he was painting the last red spoke in the wheel of a cart, he heard a sound which was made neither by the wind whistling around the crooked old roofs in the Street of Carpenters nor by a mouse nibbling within the walls. He put down his brush and got up to hunt for the source of that sound.

On the shelves around the room were arranged all the finished toys. Soldiers marched in regiments and armies; animals stood in herds and families. Rows of tiny chairs fit for doll queens' palaces were placed beside tables, chests, and curtained beds. And it was from the last and largest of these that the sound was coming.

With his paint-stained finger Master Franz looped aside the bed curtain. And there, lying on the embroidered coverlet, her hooded head half-buried in the tiny pillows, was a little lady hardly taller than the finger which disturbed her hiding place. The sound he had heard was her sobbing.

"What is this? By St. Nick himself, I must be dreaming!" burst out Master Franz, his eyes wide as he stared at the creature.

The sobs ended in a frightened gasp as the tiny head was raised, and eyes as blue as the satin of the doll queen's best court robe met his.

"I am surely dreaming! How did you get out of your box now?" He looked up at the row of fine lady dolls, each neat and tidy in her own lace-paper-edged box.

"I'm not one of your dolls, man!" answered the little thing indignantly.

"No? But then you are not a child either. You are much too

small to be one of them. Just what are you, and why should you hide in the best bed to cry?"

"I am an elf. And why am I crying?" Her little voice became a wail. "Because of this, man!" With her two hands she pulled off her hood. And there was the round ball of her head, as smooth and polished as fine ivory. There was not a single hair on it!

"So-o-o? Is that the way of it now?" Master Franz, thumb to chin, considered her thoughtfully. "Lost your wig, have you? Well, that should be a lesson to you to stay comfortably in your proper box and not stray about in this giddy way."

But at this the elf leaped down from the bed and stamped her foot.

"I tell you, man, I am NOT one of your sawdust-stuffed puppets!"

But Master Franz was no longer listening to her. Instead he pulled open a narrow drawer where, each in a compartment all its own, lay tresses of hair, hair in all colors and shades from glowing red-gold to shadeless black.

"Blue eyes," he muttered to himself. "Not brown, then, nor this yellow. Yes, we shall use black."

The elf who had been leaning over the edge of the shelf in a most perilous manner drew a deep breath.

"Why not?" she asked herself. "That old witch's spell may have wiped the hair from my head, but wearing a wig I could still go to the ball tonight. Let him continue to believe me a doll until after he has done that for me."

So she allowed Master Franz to lift her down to his

worktable, to measure and fit until she could stand it no longer, but wriggled out of his fingers to run and stare at herself in the mirror of a doll's toilet set.

"One of my best jobs, I think," said Master Franz with some pride. "Now you are even prettier than Her Majesty up yonder." He pointed to the doll queen seated haughtily on her throne on the very top shelf.

"I should think that I am!" retorted the elf. "Prettier than a puppet, indeed! But I like your work very much, toymaker, so I shall make you a gift in return. What do you want most in the world?"

"What do I want? This is a queer dream indeed. Well, I shall answer the truth to that. I wish for nothing that I do not now have in my two hands. I am very content with this shop and my work here. No, there is nothing at all for me to wish for," laughed Master Franz.

The elf frowned. "That is not a proper answer at all, man. But since you will not tell me, I shall choose for you. And now I must be off or I shall be late for the ball. Goodnight, toymaker, and see what you shall find on this table tomorrow!"

With that she disappeared and Master Franz sat blinking. He rubbed his eyes sleepily. To be sure, there were two long black hairs caught in a drop of glue on the boards before him. But of course he had been dreaming.

"Bed is the place for me. I'm too sleepy to be of use here."

He blew out his candles and went off to his bed.

* * *

When he came into the shop the next morning something lay glittering in a patch of sunlight on the worktable. It was a snuffbox of gold with a quaint design of dancing elves scrolled around its edge.

"Was I dreaming last night or not?" marvelled Master Franz. He turned the box over. "But I'm no fine gentleman to be using snuff. I do not need this." He dropped the snuffbox into one of the table drawers, and before the hour was past he had forgotten all about it.

But the happy days in the Street of Carpenters did not last. One day the King's trumpeters rode into the marketplace to proclaim war, and the men of Kammerstadt were called upon to serve in the army. Master Franz gave away the rest of the toys, laid aside his tools, and locked his shop, to put on a red coat and march away with the rest.

One cold winter's night he came home again. But there were no bright lights in the crooked-roofed houses to welcome him, only dark shadows and the driving cold of winter to bite through his worn coat and freeze the tears on his cheeks.

Only in the baker's shop was there the gleam of a candle. And Master Franz turned in there to spend his last coin for a bit of bread.

"These are hard times for us now, Master Franz. The good days are gone from Kammerstadt," the baker's wife told him. "And if you are wise, you will try your fortune elsewhere. Here the King's treasurer has sent tax gatherers to sweep up all our money, and no one has aught to spare for the buying of silly toys. A man must labor from daylight to candlelight for bare bread alone."

Franz went on to his shop. But all the magic which had once filled it was gone. Cobwebs, heavy with dust, hung from the empty shelves and he could hardly remember now how it had once looked. He crouched down beside the worktable with his aching head in his hands and there he spent the night. In the morning he opened the drawers to look for his tools but they had all been stolen long ago.

However, as he pulled open the last drawer something within it rattled. And so again he found the snuffbox. Franz could hardly believe his good fortune. Such a trinket would certainly be worth a pocketful of gold to him now. But should he, dared he, offer it for sale in Kammerstadt? Who would believe that one as ragged and poor as he had come by it honestly? He might be thrown into prison if he showed it.

It would be better to take the advice of the baker's wife. If no one in Kammerstadt would now buy toys, there were other cities where his skill might again earn his living. He had no ties to keep him fast in these ruins of his old life.

So, with the snuffbox safely hidden, Franz went out through the gates of Kammerstadt and followed the highway eastward to a new life.

He wandered from city to city, village to village. And he did not sell the snuffbox, for it seemed to him that his luck had changed from the moment he had found it. Now he was able to find work, and for some weeks he was a carpenter's helper. When he left that shop he had a new coat on his back, whole shoes on his feet, and a knapsack of supplies.

But in all his wanderings he found no city or village in which he wished to settle, or where he thought that the toymaker's craft would be truly welcomed.

After many months he came through the pass in the Gorgen Mountains and looked down upon a green and smiling land below wherein was set a fair city of many towers.

"Now I believe," said Franz to the tumbled rocks about him, "that this is the place for which I have been searching all these weary days. Here lies the city where I wish to stay."

And he set off down the mountain road at a good pace. But the city was farther off than it had appeared from the pass. At nightfall he found himself still in the wilderness, so he built a fire and grubbed in his knapsack for any bits of food he might have overlooked. His fingers found only the snuffbox. He brought it out into the firelight, turning it over and over.

"There is good gold in you," he observed. "Mayhap it will buy me proper tools and a roof to use them under. But tonight I could almost wish that you would give me food and drink."

No sooner had those words passed his lips than the snuffbox squeezed between his fingers and flew open on the moss at his feet. Before he could pick it up, a square of cloth floated out to grow and grow and spread itself with smoking dishes fit for a king's table.

At first Franz was almost afraid to eat the mysterious feast. But his hunger was greater than his caution, and he ate and drank to the last crumb. When he had done, the cloth and the dishes shrank back into the snuffbox, which then snapped shut with a click. Franz picked it up and stowed it away in his money belt.

"It would seem that I have an even greater treasure than I thought," he mused. "Will it obey my every wish or only three? That is a point I must think about, for many such gifts in past legends have been limited that way. And if that is true, I must take care as to how I spend the two still remaining."

He began to dream of all a man might wish for: wealth, a throne, the hand of the loveliest princess in the world. But none of these seemed very real to Franz. He decided that he had lived too long by the skill of his hands to care for any of them.

By noon of the next day he came to the gates of the city. But now its grim gray walls and the many angry-red and somber-black banners hanging over them did not seem inviting. The spiked gates were closed, and to enter he had to pass through a small postern and answer the many sharp questions of the sentries on duty there.

Within, the city was no pleasanter. There were many merchants' booths in the market, but the men who kept them had white, worried faces, and they all glanced back now and again over their shoulders as if an enemy might creep upon them. To Franz it was plain that this was a city where some terror ruled.

He found an inn, but when he sat down and called for ale, the little serving maid came reluctantly to bring it. As she put down his tankard she lingered a moment, scrubbing the table with her stained apron.

"Get you gone, stranger," she whispered.

"Why?"

Her face was twisted with fear as she answered. "They will be after you. No stranger enters the gates that *she* does not hear of it. And with strangers she has her sport."

"And who is she?"

"The Lady Carola, she whom the Princess Katha set over us in rule. Go quickly now, if you can, stranger. But perhaps it is already too late. And if that is so, no man or woman within these walls will raise a hand to aid you."

Franz sipped his ale. Fear he had known many times before, and never did it profit a man to turn his back upon it.

Some minutes later a file of men-at-arms tramped into the inn and ordered him to come with them. So was Franz brought to the tall keep in the very heart of the city to meet the ruler of that place.

She was neither young nor old and he could not have said whether she had beauty or was plain. But in her face and her clutching hands there were both power and evil, and Franz straightway hated her as he had never known hatred before.

"A strong man," she said harshly. "Now if you but have

wits to match your strength, it shall make our contest the more interesting for both of us."

"Our contest, Lady?"

"Aye. Since the Princess Katha thought it wise to retire from the world, I have ruled this doltish city and its teeming fools. Contests of wit and will are my only amusement. Thus shall I set you three tasks and if you cannot accomplish them—then you shall take your place among these!"

At her gesture one of the guards swept back a curtain of tapestry, and Franz saw in the wall a row of niches. In each, except for one, was a man of stone.

"Witch," returned the toymaker, "the contest you propose is an old one. There are legends in my homeland of such. But in the fullness of time there was always the same end to them."

"And that?" she prompted him.

"The witch lost."

She laughed. "If I lose, stranger, your reward shall be all the greater. But time is passing. I must set the first task before daylight is gone.

"On the top of this keep there is an eagle's nest which has been there this hundred years. And in that nest—so men say—lies the crown of an earlier ruler of this land. I have a fancy to wear that crown. Fetch it down for me, stranger!"

The guards marched Franz out into the courtyard.

"You have two hours," the captain told him sharply.

The walls of the keep were smooth stone without even hold enough for a fingernail of one who would climb. Franz slipped his hand beneath his coat and brought out the snuffbox. Now, if never again, he needed its aid.

"I wish for a way to climb the keep," he said slowly.

The box clicked open, and a thin golden vine hitched out of it. Up to the wall of the keep it crept and plastered itself against the stone, clinging as an ivy vine, growing steadily higher and higher. On this ladder Franz began to climb, not daring to look down. Up and up he followed the golden vine until at last, with aching arms, he pulled himself over the top and half tumbled, half jumped into a great mass of sticks and the bones of the eagles' prey.

Through this evil-smelling mess he combed until he found a circlet which flashed with jeweled fire. Then he trusted himself again to the vine. As he climbed down it, it shrank with his passing, so that when the stones of the courtyard were once more under his feet, the vine flowed back into the snuffbox.

But the Lady Carola had no pleasure in the crown when he offered it to her. Instead, flames of anger danced in her eyes.

"You are very clever, stranger!" Her voice was the hiss of a serpent. "Once you have won, but not twice, I think. Listen to the second task I set you:

"In the stable stands a roan mare which it is my will to ride. But since the beast is mad and attacks all who would approach it, it has never been saddled. Bring it hither gentled, stranger, and I shall believe that you have powers greater than mine!"

"So be it, Lady," replied Franz calmly.

Now Franz was city bred and knew but little of horses. However, it was plain to the most ignorant that the roan that the guards showed him was not only mad, but in its madness it was driven by a hate against all mankind. It reared and beat its hoofs against the wall, baring teeth at those who would come near it, restrained only by the heavy chains at its bridle.

"Within the hour, fool," laughed the captain, "we shall return to carry hence what is left of you."

"A most courteous act," returned Franz quietly. He waited until they had left the stable before he brought out the snuffbox.

"Give me now what will best master this demon," he asked of it.

Over the rim of the snuffbox fell a ball of rosy light which grew larger as it rolled across the floor until it lay quiet before the mare. The tall horse stood still, its eyes fixed upon the light. Franz ventured to lay a hand on a quivering flank. The horse did not move.

So did it continue to stand statue-still while Franz, with many fumblings, saddled it. Then it allowed the toymaker to lead it out, while the ball rolled before them. Thus Franz brought the mare through the crowd of awestricken men into the great hall.

At the sight of the mare, the Lady Carola shrank back in her seat. But the flames in her eyes grew, and her mouth was straight and grim.

"Twice you have won, stranger!" Her voice arose in a

harsh scream of rage. "But for you there shall be no third victory. Ten years upon ten years ago the Princess Katha went from among us, leaving this city in my hands. And no man knows whither she went. Bring her back to this high seat! That I ask of you now, little man who would match wits with me!"

For the last time Franz touched the snuffbox and muttered his wish. But nothing happened. And he knew, with a sinking heart, that three wishes only had that box held, and he had used them all. As he stood there defenseless, the Lady Carola laughed.

"So do I win! Seize him, guards!"

But Franz was desperate, and he turned to the nearest man-at-arms, snatching the spear from his hands. He hurled it swiftly, not at any who moved upon him, but at that ball of light which held the wild horse captive.

There was the tinkling of breaking crystal, and fast upon it came the scream of the mare released from the thrall the ball had laid upon her, ready to turn on them all. The Lady Carola cowered in the high seat.

"No!" she screamed. "Be as you were! Be as you were!"

And the mare was gone. In its place stood a girl with a banner of red-gold hair flying about her shoulders and a high, proud look about her such as a queen might wear.

"At last!" Her voice carried through the hall. "At last your spell is broken, Carola, and we two come to an accounting!"

To that the Lady Carola made no answer. She crouched, babbling; nor did she ever again speak a word of sense. Thus did the Princess Katha return to her city. And with her coming, the dark cloud which had held its towers in thrall was whirled away and the sun shone brightly once more in its streets and squares.

To Franz the Princess Katha offered a place at court and what honors it was in her power to bestow. But he returned a straight and honest answer.

"Liege Lady, in my hands lies my fortune. I want only to be left to use my skill as best I may."

So did there appear in that city a toy shop. And, since peace and plenty were there also, Franz indeed found the home of his dreams. By the princess' will he served upon her council, and it was often noted that when a matter of import was to be decided, Master Franz fingered a golden snuffbox until he gave his word upon the matter. It was his luck, he sometimes said.

TEDDI

J oboy was still crying when the Little used the stunner on him. Me, I had to lie there, with that tangler cord around my feet, and watch. Had to keep quiet, too. No use getting myself blasted when maybe I could still take care of Joboy.

"Take care of Joboy . . ." I'd been hearing that ever since he was born. Nats have to learn to take care early, with Little hunting packs out combing the hills and woods for them. Those packs are able to pick off the Olds early, but in the beginning, we kids aren't too much larger than the Littles, and we can hide out. We can't hide out forever, though. We have to eat, and in winter there isn't much to find in the hills—which means raiding down in Little country. Sooner or later, of course, we run into their traps, as Joboy and I did that night.

I was scared, sure, but I was more scared for Joboy. He had never been down in the fields before. I usually hid him out when I went food-snitching, but this time he had refused to stay behind. And then. . . .

All because of an old, dirty piece of fur stuffed with dried grass! I could have cried myself, only I wasn't going to let any Little see me do that. Joboy, he was just a kid, and it was his Teddi that had gotten us into this. I could see the darned thing now. One of the Littles had kicked it against the field wall, and now it sat there looking back at me, with that silly, stupid grin on its torn face.

Da had brought Teddi back to the cave when Joboy was still a baby. It was from the lowlands but not Little-made. Da told Joboy silly stories about Teddi—kid stuff, but Joboy sure liked them. After Da went out that day and never came back, Joboy wanted me to tell them, too. First I tried to remember what Da had said. Then I just added extra things out of my own head. I think Joboy thought Teddi was alive. Once, when he got torn and lost some of his insides, Joboy went wild. I stuffed Teddi with grass and tried to patch him up, but I wasn't too good at it.

Joboy carried him all the time, but that night he dropped Teddi when I found the potatoes, and when he reached for him again, he set off the alarm, and the Littles were right on us.

They used a tangler on me quick. Guess they must have known I was a raider and knew most of the tricks. I told Joboy to beat it, and he might have gotten away if he hadn't tried to get Teddi again. So there we were; the Littles had us, but good.

Now they stood around us, looking us over as if we were animals. I guess, to the Littles, that's what we Nats were. I wondered if they knew just how much we hated them! Littles—I could have spit right in their nasty, screwed-up faces. Only I didn't—not when they had Joboy and maybe would make him pay for what I did.

There were only six of them. Put me on my feet, free, and I could— But I knew I couldn't, ever. They had tanglers and stunners. What did we have? Stones and sticks. Da had had a gun but nothing left to shoot out of it. It was at the back of our cave now, leaning against the wall, not as much good as a well-shaped club would be.

The six of them were wearing the green suits of a hunting pack. They had come down on us in one of their copters. The Littles have everything—cars, planes, you name it—but we can't use them; they're all too small. Maybe Joboy could squeeze into the pilot's seat in a copter, but he wouldn't know how to fly it.

Joboy lay there as if he were dead, but he was only stunned—so far. I tried not to guess what they would do to us. We were Nats, and that made us things to be hunted down and gotten rid of.

A Little walked over to me and looked right down into my eyes. His eyes were cold and hard, like his face. Yet once we were the same, Littles and Nats. They never seem to think of that, and I guess we don't much, either.

"You, Nat"—he nudged my shoulder with the toe of his boot—"where's your filthy nest? Any more of you back there?" I'm sure he didn't expect any answer. If he had dealt with us before, he should have known he would get none.

Da warned us long ago not to team up with any other Nats. More than one family of us together was easy hunting. Most of us stayed on our own. We were cautious about meeting strange Nats, too. Sometimes the Littles had tame Nats—ones they could control—sent into the hill country to nose us out. However, no Nat ever spilled to the Littles unless he was brain-emptied, so the less we knew, the better. They might backtrack us to the cave, but that wouldn't do them any good. Da had been gone since last winter, and Mom, though I still remembered her, had died of the coughing sickness when Joboy was only a baby. Maybe they would find Da's hiding places and the books, but that didn't matter much at this point. They had us, and there was no escaping from a Nat pen, once you were dumped in. Or was there? You heard stories, and I could keep my eyes and ears open. . . .

"No more of us," I told him truthfully. "Just Joboy and me."

He made a face as if I smelled bad. "Two's two too many. Sent for the pickup yet, Max?" He spoke to the one putting his stunner back in his belt after he had attended to Joboy.

"On its way, chief."

I wondered if I should cry a bit, let them see me scared. But then they might stun me, too. Better be quiet and try to find a way to— But there was no way. When I realized that, it was like really having the stunner knock me out, only I wasn't able to sleep. I had to lie and think about it.

They didn't pay me any more attention, because they didn't have to; that tangler held me as if I were shut up in a cave, with a rock too big to push filling the entrance. One of them wandered over to Teddi, laughed, and kicked him. Teddi sailed up in the air and came right apart at a seam. I was glad Joboy didn't see that, and I hated them worse than ever. I hated until I was all hate and nothing else.

Pretty soon one of their trucks came along. The two men in the front got out. We were picked up, gingerly, as if the Littles hated even to touch us, and dumped in the back. I landed hard and it hurt, and I was glad Joboy couldn't feel it when he landed.

I had time to think as the truck ran along through the night, heading for one of their cities—cities that had once been ours, too. How long ago? I wondered.

Da could read the books. He could write, too. He made Joboy and me learn. Once he said that the Littles thought we were no better than animals, but that there was no need for us to prove them right. He made us learn about the past, as much as he knew.

Littles began quite a while back, when there were too many people in the world. The people built too many houses and too many roads, ate too much, and covered all the country. A lot of people began to worry, and they had different ideas as to what could help. The cities, especially, were traps, overpopulated and full of bad air.

None of their ideas seemed to work—until they started on the Littles. They found a way to work on a person's body, even before he was born, so that he started life a lot smaller and never did grow very big. His children were small, too, and so it went, on and on. The big cities now could house more and more people. They didn't have to build more and bigger roads, because the cars were made smaller and smaller, to match the Littles. Littles didn't need so much food, either, so less land was needed to produce what was required.

There were some people, however, who thought this was all wrong, and they refused to take the treatment to make their children little. When the government passed laws that said everyone *had* to be a Little, the Naturals—the Nats—moved to places where they thought they could hide. Then the Littles began to hunt them.

Da's people, way back, had been leaders against the idea of making Littles, because they had found out that being little began to change the way people thought, made them hate everyone not just like themselves. Da said they were "conditioned" to have the ideas that those who were in power wanted them to have—like being a Little was the right way to live and being a Natural was like being a killer or a robber or something. Da said people had worked and fought and even died to let everyone have an equal chance in life, and now the Littles were starting the old, bad ways of thinking, all over again—only this time they were even worse.

That's why he held on to the old books and made us learn all about what had happened, so we could tell our children—

though we probably wouldn't ever get to tell anyone anything now. I shivered as I bumped around in that truck, wondering what the Littles were going to do with us. They couldn't make us Littles, so what *did* they do with Nats when they caught them?

First they dumped us in a Nat pen. It was a big room, with walls like stone. Its small windows were so far up that there was no way to reach them. Along the walls were benches, squat and low, to match Littles and no one else. It smelled bad, as if people had been shut up there for a long time, and I guess people like us had been. To the Littles, of course, we weren't people—just things.

When the Littles brought us in, they had stunners out, and they yelled to the others to get away from the door or they would ray. They threw us on the floor, and then one sprayed the tangler cords so they began to dissolve. By the time I was free, the Littles were gone. I crawled over to Joboy. Crawl was all I could do, I had been tied up so long. Joboy was still sleeping. I sat beside him and looked at the others in the pen.

There were ten of them, all kids. A couple were just babies, and they were crying. The only one as old as me was a girl. She held one of the babies, trying to get it to suck a wet rag, but she looked over its head at me mighty sharp. There were two other girls. The rest were boys.

"Tam?" Joboy opened his eyes. "Tam!" He was scared.

"I'm here!" I put my hands on him so he'd know it was the truth. Joboy had a lot of bad dreams. Sometimes he woke up scared, and I had to make him sure I was right there.

"Tam, where are we?" He caught at one of my hands with both of his and held it fast.

One of the boys laughed. "Look around, kid, just look around."

He was smaller than me, but now I saw he was older than I first thought. I didn't like his looks; he seemed too much like a Little.

He could be a "tweener." Some of the Little kids were what they called "throwbacks." They grew too big, so their people were ashamed and afraid of them and got rid of them. I guess they were afraid the tweeners might start everyone changing in size if they kept them around. The tweeners hated Nats, too—maybe even more, because they were something like them.

The girl with the baby spoke. "Shut up, Raul." Then she asked me, "Kinfolk?"

"Brothers." That Raul might be older, but I thought this girl was the head one there. "I'm Tam, and this is Joboy."

She nodded. "I'm El-Su. She's Amay." She motioned toward another girl, about Joboy's age, I reckoned, who had moved up beside her. "We're sisters. The rest. . . ." She said who they were, but I didn't try to remember their names. They were mostly just dirty faces and ragged clothes.

I ran my tongue over my lips, but before I could ask any questions, Joboy jerked at my hand. "Tam, I'm hungry. Please, Tam—"

"What about it?" I turned to El-Su. "Do we get fed?"

She pointed to the other wall. "Sure. They don't starve

us—at least, not yet. Go over there and press that red button. Be ready to catch what comes out, or it ends up on the floor."

I did as she told me, and it was a good thing she had warned me. As it was, I nearly didn't catch the pot of stuff. I took it over to one of the benches, Joboy tailing me. There were no spoons, so we had to eat with our fingers. The food was stewed stuff that didn't taste like much of anything, but we were hungry enough to scrape it all out. While we ate, the rest stood around watching us, as if they had nothing else to do—which was the truth.

When I had finished, I tried El-Su again.

"So they feed us. What else do they do? What do they want us for?"

Raul moved in between us and answered first. "Make you work, big boy—really make you work. Bet they haven't had one as big as you for a long time." He used the word "big" the way a Little does, meaning something nasty.

"Work how?" The Littles had machines to do their work, and those machines were made for Littles, not Nats, to run.

"You'll see—" Raul began, but El-Su, holding the baby, who had gone to sleep against her shoulder, reached out her other hand and gave him a push.

"He's asking me, *little* one." Now she made "little" sound nasty, in return. "They indenture us," she told me.

"Indenture?" That was a new word, and anything new, connected with Littles, could be bad. The sooner I knew how bad, the better.

She watched me closely, as if she thought I was pretending I didn't know what she meant.

"You never heard?"

I was short in answering. "If I had, would I be asking?"

"Right." El-Su nodded. "You must have been picked up down south. Well, it's like this. The Littles, they're sending ships up in the sky—way off to the stars—"

"Moon walk!" One of Da's books had pictures about that.

"Farther out." This El-Su spoke as if she had had old books to read, too. "Clear to another sun with a lot of worlds. To save space on the ship, they put most of the people to sleep—freeze them—until they get there."

Maybe if I hadn't read that book of Da's, I would have thought she was making all this up out of her head, the way I made up the stories about Teddi for Joboy. But that moon book had some talk in it about star travel, also.

"The Littles found a world out there, like this one. But it's all wild—no cities, no roads, nothing—just lots of trees and country, where no one has ever been. They want to live there, but they can't take their digging and building machines along. Those are too heavy; besides, they'd take up too much room in the ship. So they want to take Nats—like us—to do the work. They get rid of grown-up Nats when they bring them here, but they aren't so afraid of kids. Maybe we're lucky." El-Su didn't sound so sure about that, however.

"Yeah." Raul pushed ahead of her again. "You got to work and do just what a Little tells you to. And you'll never get back here, neither—not in your whole life! What do you think of that, big boy?"

I didn't think much of it, but I wasn't going to say so—not when Joboy had tight hold of my hand.

"Tam, are they really going to shoot us up into the sky?" he asked.

He didn't sound scared, as I thought he might be. He just looked interested when I glanced down at him. Joboy gets interested in things . . . likes to sit and study them. Back in the woods, he would watch bugs, for what seemed like hours, and then tell me what they were doing and why. Maybe he made it all up, but it sounded real. And he could chitter like a squirrel or whistle like a bird, until the animals would actually come to him.

"I don't know," I said, but I had no reason to doubt that both El-Su and Raul *thought* they were telling the truth.

It seemed that they *were,* from what happened to us: After we had been there a couple of days, some Littles started processing us. That's what they called it—processing. We had to get scrubbed up, and they stuck us with needles. That hurt, but there was no getting back at them. Some of them had stunners, and even blasters, on us every minute. They never told us anything. That made it bad, because you kept thinking that something worse yet was waiting.

Then they divided the group. El-Su, Amay, and another girl, called Mara, Raul, Joboy, and me they kept together. I made up my mind that if they tried to take Joboy, stunner or no, I was going to jump the nearest Little. Perhaps the Littles guessed they would have trouble if they tried to separate us.

Finally they marched us into a place where there were boxes on the floor and ordered each of us to get into one. I was afraid for Joboy, but he didn't cry or hold back. He had that interested look on his face, and he even smiled at me. It gave me a warm feeling that he wasn't scared. I was—plenty!

We got into the boxes and lay down, and then, almost immediately, we went to sleep. I don't remember much, and I never knew how long we were in those boxes. For a while I dreamed. I was in a place all sunny and full of flowers with nice smells and lots of other happy things. There was Joboy, and he was walking hand in hand (or *paw* in hand) with Teddi. In that place, Teddi was as big as Joboy, and he was alive, as I think Joboy always thought he was.

They were talking without sounds—like just in their heads —and I could hear them, too. I can't remember what they were saying, except that it was happy talk. And I felt light and free, a way I couldn't remember ever feeling before—as if, in this place, you didn't have to be afraid of Littles or their traps. Joboy turned to look back at me, with a big smile on his face.

"Teddi knows. Teddi *always* knows," he said.

I hurt. I hurt all over. I hurt so bad I yelled; at least, somebody was yelling. I opened my eyes, and everything was all red, like fire, and that hurt, too—and so I woke up on a new world.

When we could walk (we were so stiff, it hurt to move at all), the Littles, four of them with blasters, herded us into another room, where the walls were logs of wood and the floor was dirt, tramped down hard. They made us take a bunch of pills, and we moved around, but there were no windows to see out of.

After a while, they came for us again and marched us out into the open. We knew then that we were on another world, all right.

The sky was *green*, not blue, and there were queer-looking trees and bushes. Right around the log-walled places, the ground had been burned off or dug up until it was typically ugly Little country. They had a couple of very small, light diggers and blasters, and they ran these around, trying to make the ugly part bigger.

We marched across to a place where there was just grass growing. There the Little chief lined us up and said this grass had to be dug out and cleared away so seeds could be planted, to test whether they could grow things from our world. He had tools (they must have been made for tweeners, at least, because they were all right for us): shovels, picks, hoes. He told us to get to work.

It was tough going. The grass roots ran deep, and we couldn't get much of the ground scraped as bare as he wanted it. They had to give us breaks for rest and food. I guess they didn't want to wear us out too fast.

While we weren't working, I took every chance to look around. Once you got used to the different colors of things, it wasn't so strange. There was one thing, I think, that the Littles should have remembered better. We Nats had lived in the woods and wild places for a long time. We were used to trees and bushes. The Littles never liked to go very far into the wild places; they needed walls about them to feel safe and happy— if Littles could be happy.

So the wide bigness of this wild country must have scared the Littles. It bothered me, just because it was unfamiliar, but not as much as it bothered the Littles. I had a feeling that, if what lay beyond that big stand of trees was no worse than what was right here, there was no reason why we Nats couldn't take to the woods the first chance we got. Then let the Littles just try to find us! I chewed on that in my mind but didn't say it out loud—yet.

It was on the fifth day of working that Raul, Joboy, and I were sent, along with a small clearing machine, in the other direction—into the woods on the opposite side of that bare place. I noticed that Joboy kept turning his head in one direction. When our guard dropped back, he whispered to me.

"Tam, Teddi's here!"

I missed a step. Teddi! Teddi was a dirty rag! Was Joboy hurt in the head now? I was so scared that I could have yelled, but Joboy shook his head at me.

"Teddi says no. He'll come when it's time. He don't like the Littles. They make everything bad."

They set us to piling up logs and tree branches. We could lift and carry bigger loads than any Little. I kept Joboy with me as much as I could, and away from Raul. I didn't want Raul to know about Joboy and Teddi. As far as I was concerned, Raul still had some of the tweener look, and I never trusted him.

There was sticky sap oozing out of the wood, and it got all over us. At first I tried to wipe it off Joboy and myself, using leaves, but Joboy twisted away from me.

"Don't, Tam. Leave it on. It makes the bugs stay away."

I had noticed that the Littles kept slapping at themselves and grunting. There were a lot of flies, and from the way the Littles acted, they could really bite. But the buzzers weren't bothering us, so I was willing to stay sticky, if that's what helped. The Littles acted as if the bites were getting worse. They moved away from us. Finally two of them went back to the log buildings, to get bug spray, I suppose, leaving only the one who drove the machine. He got into the small cab and closed the windows. I suppose he thought there was no chance of our running off into that strange wilderness.

Raul sat down to rest, but Joboy wandered close to the edge of the cut, and I followed to keep an eye on him. He squatted down near a bush, facing it. The leaves were big and flat and had yellow veins. Joboy stared, as if they were windows he could see through.

I knelt beside him. "What is it, Joboy?"

"Teddi's there." He pointed with his chin, not moving his scratched, dirty hands from his knees.

"Joboy—" I began, then stopped suddenly. In my head was something, not words but a feeling, like saying hello, except— Oh, I can never tell just how it was!

"Teddi," Joboy said. His voice was like Da's, when I was no older than Joboy and there was a bad storm and Da was telling me not to be afraid.

What made that come into my mind? I stared at the bush. As I studied it now, I saw an opening between two of the leaves that *was* a window, enough for me to see—

Teddi! Well, perhaps not Teddi as Da had first brought him (and before Joboy wore him dirty and thin from much loving) but enough like him to make Joboy know. Only this was no stuffed toy; this was a live creature! And it was fully as large as Joboy himself, which was about as big as one of the Littles. Its bright eyes stared straight into mine.

Again I had that feeling of greeting, of meeting someone who meant no harm, who was glad to see me. I had no doubt that this was a friend. But—what was it? The Littles hated wild things, especially *big* wild things. They would kill it! I glanced back at the one in the cab, almost sure I would see him aiming a blaster at the bush.

"Joboy," I said as quietly as I could, "the Little will—"

Joboy smiled and shook his head. "The Little won't hurt Teddi, Tam. Teddi will help us; he likes us. He *thinks* to me how he likes us."

"What you looking at, kid?" Raul called.

Joboy pointed to a leaf. "The buzzer. See how big that one is?"

Sure enough, there was an extra-big one of the red buzzing flies sitting on the leaf, scraping its front legs together and looking as if it wanted a bite of someone. At that moment, I felt

Teddi leave, which made me happier, as I didn't have Joboy's confidence in Teddi's ability to defend himself against the Littles.

That was the beginning. Whenever we went near the woods, sooner or later Teddi would turn up in hiding. I seldom saw any part of him, but I always felt him come and go. Joboy seemed to be able to *think* with him and exchange information—until the day Teddi was caught.

The creature had always been so cautious that I had begun to believe that the Littles would never know about him. But suddenly he walked, on his hind legs, right into the open. Raul yelled and pointed, and the Little on guard used his stunner. Teddi dropped. At least, he hadn't been blasted, not that that would necessarily save him.

I expected Joboy to go wild, but he didn't. He went over with the rest of us to see Teddi, lying limp and yellow on mashed, sticky leaves where we had been taking off tree limbs. Joboy acted as if he didn't know a thing about him. That I could not understand.

Teddi was a little taller than Joboy. His round, furry head would just top my shoulder, and his body was plump and fur-covered all over. He had large, round ears, set near the top of his head, a muzzle that came to a point, and a dark brown button of a nose. Yes, he looked like an animal, but I was sure he was something far different.

Now he was just a stunned prisoner, and the Littles made us carry him over to the machine. Then they took us all back to camp. They dumped us in the lockup and took Teddi into another hut. I know what Littles do to animals. They might— I only hoped Joboy couldn't imagine what the Littles might do to Teddi. I still didn't understand why he wasn't upset.

But when we were shut in, he took my hand. "Tam?"

I thought I knew what he was going to ask—that I help Teddi—and there was nothing I could do.

"Tam, listen—Teddi, he wanted to be caught. He did! He has a plan for us. It will work only if he gets real close to the Littles, so he had to be caught."

"What does he mean?" El-Su demanded.

"The kid's mind-broke!" Raul burst out. "They knocked over some kind of an animal out there and—"

"Shut up!" I snapped at Raul. I had to know what Joboy meant, because it was plain that he believed what he was saying, and he knew far more about Teddi than I did.

"Teddi can do things with his head." Joboy paid no attention to either El-Su or Raul, looking straight at me as if he must make me believe what he was saying.

Remembering for myself, I could agree in part. "I know—"

"He can make them—the Littles—feel bad inside. But we have to help."

"How? We can't get out of here—"

"Not yet," Joboy agreed. "But we have to help Teddi think—"

"Mind-broke!" Raul exploded and slouched away. But El-Su and the other two girls squatted down to listen.

"How do we help think?" She asked the question already on my tongue.

"You feel afraid. Remember all the bad things you are afraid of. And we hold hands in a circle to remember them—like bad dreams." Joboy was plainly struggling to find words to make us understand.

"That's easy enough—to remember bad things," El-Su agreed. "All right, we think. Come on, girls." She took Amay's hand and Mara's. I took Mara's other hand, and Joboy took Amay's, so we were linked in a circle.

"Now"—Joboy spoke as sharply as any Little setting us to work—"think!"

We had plenty of bad things to remember: cold, hunger, fear. Once you started thinking and remembering, it all heaped up into a big black pile of bad things. I thought about every one of them—how Mom died, how Da was lost, and how—and how—and how. . . .

I got so I didn't even see where we were or whose hands I held. I forgot all about the present; I just sat and remembered and remembered. It came true again in my mind, as if it were happening all over again, until I could hardly stand it. Yet once I had begun, I had to keep on.

Far off, there was a noise. Something inside me tried to push that noise away. I had to keep remembering, feeding a big black pile. Then suddenly the need for remembering was gone. I awakened from the nightmare.

I could hear someone crying. El-Su was facing me with tear streaks on her grimy face; the two little girls were bawling out loud. But Joboy wasn't crying. He stood up, looking at the door, though he still held on to our hands.

Then I looked in that direction. Raul crouched beside the door, hands to his head, moaning as if something hurt him bad. The door was opening—probably a Little, to find out why we were making all that noise.

Teddi stood there, with another Teddi behind him, looking over his shoulder. All the blackness was gone out of my head, as if I had rid myself of all the bad that had ever happened to me in my whole life. I felt so light and free and happy—as if I could flap my arms like wings and go flying off!

Outside, near where the Teddis stood, there was a Little crawling along the ground, holding on to his head the way Raul did. He didn't even see us as we walked past him. We saw two other Littles, one lying quiet, as if he were dead. Nobody tried to stop us or the Teddis. We just walked out of the bad old life together.

I don't know how long we walked before we came to an open place, and I thought, *This I remember, because it was in my dream.* Here were Joboy and Teddi, hand in paw. There was a Teddi with me, too, his furry paw in my hand, and from him the feeling was all good.

We understand now what happened and why. When the Littles first came to this world, spoiling and wrecking, as they always have done and still do, the Teddis tried to stop them. But the minds of the Littles were closed tight; the Teddis could not reach them—not until they found Joboy. He had no fear of them, because he knew a Teddi who had been a part of his life.

So Joboy was the key to unlock the Littles' minds, with us to add more strength, just as it takes more than one to lift a really big stone. With Joboy and us opening the closed doors of the Littles' minds, the Teddis could feed back to them all the fear they had spread through the years, the fear we had lived with and known in our nightmares. Such fear was a poison worse than any of the Littles' own weapons.

We still go and *think* at them now and then, with a Teddi to aim our thoughts from where we hide. From all the signs, it won't be long before they will have had enough and will raise their starship and leave us alone. Maybe they will try to come back, but by then, perhaps, the Teddis and we can make it even harder for them.

Now we are free, and no one is ever going to put us back in a Nat pen. We are not "Nats" anymore. That is a Little name, and we take nothing from the Littles—ever again! We have a new name from old, old times. Once it was a name to make little people afraid, so it is our choice. We are free, and we are *Giants*, growing larger every day.

So shall we stay!

DESIRABLE LAKESIDE
RESIDENCE

*I went to the river
to drown all my sorrow
But the river was more
to be pitied than I . . .*

—*Scots ballad*

Her face felt queer and light without her respirator on—almost like being out here without any clothes. Jill thumbed the worn cords of her breather, crinkling them, smoothing them out again, without paying attention to what her hands were doing, her eyes were so busy surveying this new, strange and sometimes terrifying outer world.

Back home had been the apartment, sealed, of course, and the school, with the sealed bus in between. Sometimes there had been a visit to the shopping center. But she could hardly really remember now. Even the trip to this place was rather like a dream.

Movement in the long ragged grass beyond the end of the concrete block on which Jill sat. She tensed—

A black head, a small furred head with two startling blue eyes—

Jill hardly dared to breathe even though there was no smog at all. Those eyes were watching her measuringly. Then a sinuous black body flowed into full view. One minute it had not been there, the next—it just was!

This was—she remembered the old books—a cat!

Dogs and cats, people had had them once, living in their houses. Before the air quotient got so low no one was allowed to keep a pet in housing centers. But there was no air quotient here yet—a cat could live—

Jill studied the cat, sitting up on its haunches, its tail laid straight out on the ground behind it, just the very tip of that twitching a little now and then. Except for that one small movement it might have been a pretend cat, like the old pretend bear she had when she was little. Very suddenly it yawned wide, showing sharp white teeth, a curling pink tongue, bright in color, against the black which was all the rest of it.

"Hello, cat—" Jill said in that quiet voice which the bigness of Outside caused her to use.

Black ears twitched as if her words had tickled them a little. The cat blinked.

"Do you live here—Outside?" she asked. Because here things did dare to live Outside. She had seen a bird that very morning, and in the grass were all kinds of hoppers and crawlers. "It's nice"—Jill was gaining confidence—"to live Outside—but sometimes," she ended truthfully, "scary, too. Like at night."

"Ulysses, where are you, cat?"

Jill jumped. The cat blinked again, turned its head to look back over one shoulder. Then it uttered a small sound.

"I heard you, Ulysses. Now where are you?"

There was a swishing in grass and bush. Jill gathered her feet under her for a quick takeoff. Yet she had no intention of retreat until that was entirely necessary.

The bushes parted and Jill saw another girl no bigger than she was. She settled back on her chosen seat. The cat arose and went to rub back and forth against the newcomer's scratched and sandy legs.

"Hello," Jill ventured.

"You're Colonel Baylor's niece." The other made that sound almost like an accusation. She stood with her hands bunched into fists resting on her hips. As Jill, she wore a one-piece shorts-tunic, but hers was a rusty green which seemed to melt into the coloring of the bushes. Jill had an odd feeling that if the other chose she could be unseen while still standing right there.

Her skin was brown and her hair fluffed out around her face in an upstanding black puff.

"He's my uncle Shaw," Jill offered. "Do—do you live Outside, too?"

"Outside," the other repeated as if the word were strange. "Sure, I live here. Me—I'm Marcy Scholar. I live over there." She pivoted to point to her left. "The other way's the lake—or what used to be the lake. My dad—when I was just a little old baby—he used to go fishing there. You believe me?"

She eyed Jill challengingly as if expecting a denial.

Jill nodded. She could believe anything of Outside. It had already shown her so many wonders which before had existed only in books, or on the screen of the school TV they used when Double Smog was so bad you couldn't even use the sealed buses.

"You come from up North, the bad country—" Marcy took a step forward. "The colonel, he has a big pull with the government or you couldn't get here at all. We don't allow people coming into a Clear. It might make it bad, too, if too many came. Bad enough with the lakes all dead, and the rest of it."

Jill's eyes suddenly smarted as badly as they did once when she was caught in a room where the breather failed. She did not want to remember why she was here.

"Uncle Shaw walked on the moon! The President of the whole United States gave him a medal for it. He's in the history books—" she countered. "I guess what Uncle Shaw wants, he gets."

Marcy did not protest as Jill half expected. Instead she nodded. "That's right. My father—he worked on the Project, too, that's how come we live here. When they closed down the big base and said no more space flights, well, we moved here with the colonel, and Dr. Wilson, and the Pierces. Look here—"

She pushed past Jill and swept away some of the foliage. Behind those trailing, yellowish leaves, was a board planted on a firm stake in the ground; on it, very faint lettering.

"You read that?" Marcy stabbed a finger at the words.

"Sure I can read!" Jill studied the almost lost lines. "It says, 'Desirable Lakeside Residence.'"

"And that's what all this was!" Marcy answered. "Once— years and years ago—people paid lots of money for this land—land beside a lake. Of course, that was before all the fish, and turtles and alligators and things died off, and the water was all full of weeds. You can hardly tell where the lake was any more—come on—I'll show you!"

Jill eyed the mass of rusty green doubtfully. But Marcy hooked back an armful to show an opening beyond. And, at that moment, Ulysses came to life in flowing movement and disappeared through it. Fastening her respirator to her belt, Jill followed.

It was like going through a tunnel, but the walls of this tunnel were alive, not concrete. She put out a hand timidly now and then to touch fingertips to leaves, springy branches, all the parts of Outside. Then they were out of the tunnel, before them what seemed to be a smooth green surface some distance below where they now stood. However, as she studied it, Jill could see there were brown patches which the green did not cover and which looked liquid.

This was very different from any lake in a picture, but then everything was different now from pictures. Old people kept talking about how it was when they were young, saying, yes, the pictures were right. But sometimes Jill wondered if they were not just trying to remember it and getting the pictures mixed up with what they wanted to believe. Perhaps the pictures were stories which were never true, even long ago.

Marcy shaded her eyes with her hand, stared out across the green-brown surface.

"That's funny—"

"What's funny?"

"Seems like there is more water showing today—like the weeds are gone. Maybe it's so poisoned now even the old weeds can't live in it." She picked up a stick from the ground by her feet, and then lay full length to reach over and plunge the end of it into the thick mass below, dragging it back and forth.

Ulysses appeared again. Not up with them, but below. Jill could see him crouched on a slime-edged stone. His head was forward as he stared into the weeds, as if he could see something the girls could not.

"Hey!" Marcy braced herself up on her elbows. "Did you see that?"

"What?"

"When I poked this old stick in right here"—she leaned forward to demonstrate—"something moved away—along there!" She used the stick as a pointer. "Watch Ulysses, he must have seen it too!"

The cat's tail swept back and forth; he was clearly gazing in the direction Marcy indicated.

"You said all the fish, the turtles and things are dead." Jill edged back. Once there had been snakes, too. Were the snakes dead?

"Sure are. My dad says nothing could live in this old lake! But something did move away. Let's see—" She wormed her way along, striking at the leaves below, cutting swaths through them, leaving the growth tattered. But, though they both watched intently, there were no more signs of anything which might or might not be fleeing the lashing branch.

"Bug—a big bug?" suggested Jill as Marcy rolled back, dropping the stick.

"Sure would be a *big* one." Marcy sounded unconvinced. "You going to live here—all the time?"

Jill began to twist at her respirator again. "I guess so."

"What's it like up North, in the bad country?"

Jill looked about her a little desperately. Outside was so different, how could she tell Marcy about Inside? She did not even want to remember those last black days.

"They—they cut down on our block quota," she said in a rush. "Two of the big breathers burned out. People were all jammed together in the part where the conditioners still worked. But there were too many. They—they took old Mr. Evans away and Mrs. Evans, too. Daddy—somehow he got a message to Uncle Shaw, and he sent for me. But Daddy couldn't come. He is one of the maintainers, and they aren't allowed even to leave their own sections for fear something will happen and the breathers break down."

Marcy was watching her narrowly.

"I bet you're glad to be here."

"I don't know—it's all so different, it's Outside." Now Jill looked around her wildly. That stone where she had sat, from it she could turn around and see the house. From here—now all she could see were bushes. Where was the house—?

She got to her feet, shaking with the cold inside her.

"Please"—somehow she got out that plea—"where's the house? Which way did we come to get here?" Inside was safe—

"You frightened? Nothing to be frightened of. Just trees and things. And Ulysses, but he's a friend. He's a smart cat, understands a lot you say. If he could only talk now—" Marcy leaned over and called:

"Ulysses, you come on up. Nothing to catch down there, no use your pretending there is."

Jill was still shaking a little. But Marcy's relaxation was soothing. And she wanted to see the cat close again. Perhaps he would let her pet him.

Again that black head pushed through the brush and Ulysses, stopping once to lick at his shoulder, came to join them.

"He's half Siamese," Marcy announced as if that made him even more special. "His mother is Min-Hoy. My mother had her since a little kitten. She's old now and doesn't go out much. Listen, you got a cat?"

Jill shook her head. "They don't allow them—nothing that uses up air, people have to have it all. I never saw one before, except in pictures."

"Well, suppose I let you have half of Ulysses—"

"Half?"

"Sure, like you take him some days, and me some. Ulysses"—she looked to the cat. "This is Jill Baylor, she never had a cat. You can be with her sometimes, can't you?"

Ulysses had been inspecting one paw intently. Now he looked first at Marcy as if he understood every word, and then turned his head to apply the same searching stare to Jill. She knelt and held out her hand.

"Ulysses—"

He came to her with the grave dignity of his species, sniffed at her fingers, then rubbed his head back and forth against her flesh, his silky soft fur like a caress.

"He likes you." Marcy nodded briskly. "He'll give you half his time, just wait and see!"

"*Jill!*" a voice called from nearby.

Marcy stood up. "That's your aunt, you'd better go. Miss Abby's a great one for people being prompt."

"I know. How—how do I go?"

Marcy guided her back through the green tunnel. Ulysses disappeared again. But Marcy stayed to where Aunt Abby stood under the roof overhang. Jill was already sure that her aunt liked that house a great deal better before Jill came to stay in it.

"Where have you been—? Oh, hello, Marcy. You can tell your mother the colonel got the jeep fixed and I'm going in to town later this afternoon, if she wants a shopping lift."

"Yes, Mrs. Baylor." Marcy was polite but she did not linger. There was no sign of Ulysses.

Nobody asked Jill concerning her adventures of the morning and she did not volunteer. She was uneasy with Aunt Abby; as for Uncle Shaw, she thought most of the time he did not even know she was there. Sometimes he seemed to come back from some far distance and talk to her as if she were a baby. But most of the time he was shut up at the other end of the house in a room Aunt Abby had warned her not to enter. What it contained she had no idea.

There were only four families now living by the lake, she was to discover. Marcy's, the Haddams, who were older and seemed to spend most of their time working in a garden trying to raise things. Though Marcy reported most of the stuff died off before it ever got big or ripe enough to eat, but they kept on trying. Then there were the Williamses and they—Marcy warned her to stay away from them, even though Jill had no desire to explore Outside alone. The Williamses, Marcy reported, were dirt-mean, dirt-dirty, and wrong in the head. Which was enough to frighten Jill away from any contact.

But it was the Williamses who caused all the rumpus the night of the full moon.

Jill awakened out of sleep and sat up in her bed, her heart thumping, her body beginning to shake as she heard that awful screaming. It came from Outside, awakening all the suspicions her days with Marcy had lulled. Then she heard sounds in the house, Uncle Shaw's heavy tread, Aunt Abby's voice.

The generator was off again and they had had only lamps for a week. But she saw through the window the broad beam of a flashlight cut the night. Then she heard Marcy's father call from the road and saw a second flashlight.

There was another shriek and Jill cried out, too, in echo. The door opened on Aunt Abby, who went swiftly to the window, pulling it closed in spite of the heat.

"It's all right." She sat down on the bed and took Jill's hands in hers. "Just some animal—"

But Jill knew better. There weren't many animals—Ulysses, Min-Hoy, the old mule the Haddams kept. Marcy had told her all the wild animals were gone.

There was no more screaming and Aunt Abby took her into bed with her so after a while Jill did sleep. When she went for breakfast, Uncle Shaw was in his usual place. Nobody said anything about what had happened in the night and she felt she must not ask. It was not until she met Marcy that she heard the story.

"Beeny Williams," Marcy reported, "clean out of his head and running down the road yelling demons were going to get him. My father had to knock him out. They're taking him in town to a doctor." She stopped and looked sidewise at Jill in an odd kind of way as if she were in two minds whether to say something or not. Then she asked abruptly:

"Jill, do you ever dream about—well, some queer things?"

"What kind of things?" Everyone had scary dreams.

"Well, like being in a green place and moving around—not like walking, but sort of flying. Or being away from that green place and wanting a lot to get back."

Jill shook her head. "You dream like that?"

"Sometimes—only usually you never remember the dreams plain when you wake up, but these you do. It seems to be important. Oh, stuff!" She threw up her hands. "Dad says to stay away from the lake. Seems Beeny went wading in a piece of it last night, might be he got some sort of poison. But all those Williamses are crazy. I don't see how wading in the lake could do anything to him. Dad didn't say we couldn't walk around it, let's go see—"

They took the familiar way through the tunnel. Jill blinked in the very bright sun. Then she blinked again.

"Marcy, there's a lot more water showing! See—there and there! Perhaps your dad is right, could be something killing off the weeds."

"Sure true. Ulysses," she called to the cat crouched on the stone below, "you come away from there, could be you might catch something bad."

However Ulysses did not so much as twitch an ear this time in response—nor did he come. Marcy threatened to climb down and get him, but Jill pointed out that the bank was crumbling and she might land in the forbidden lake.

They left the cat and worked their way along the shore, coming close to a derelict house well embowered in the skeletons of dead creepers and feebler shoots of new ones.

"Spooky," Marcy commented. "Looks like a place where things could hide and jump out—"

"Who used to live there, I wonder?"

"Dr. Wilson. He was at the Cape, too. And he walked on the moon—"

"Dr. Morgan Wilson." Jill nodded. "I remember."

"He was the worst upset when they closed down the Project 'cause he was right in the middle of an experiment. Tried to bring his stuff along here and work on it, but he didn't have any more money from the government and nobody would listen to him. He never got over feeling bad about it. One night he just up and walked out into the lake—just like that!" Marcy waved a hand. "They never found him until the next morning. And you know what—he took a treasure with him—and it was never found."

"A treasure—what?"

"Well, he had these moon rocks he was using in his experiment. He'd picked them up himself. My dad said they used to keep them in cases where people could go and see them. But after New York and Chicago and Los Angeles all went dead in the Breakdown and there was no going to the moon any more—nor money to spend except for breathers and fighting the poison and all—nobody cared what became of a lot of old rocks. So these were lost in the lake."

"What did they look like?"

"Oh, I guess like any old rock. They were just treasures because they came from another world."

They turned back then for they were faced with a palmetto thicket which they could not penetrate. It was a lot hotter and Jill began to think of indoors and the slight cool one could find by just getting out of the sun.

"Come on home with me," she urged. "We can have some lemonade and Aunt Abby gave me a big old catalogue—we can pick out what we'd like to buy if they still had the store and we had any money."

Wish buying was usually a way to spend a rainy day, but it might also fill up a hot one.

"Okay."

So they were installed on Jill's bed shortly, turning the limp pages of the catalogue and rather listlessly making choices, when there was a scratching at the outside door just beyond the entrance to Jill's bedroom.

"Hey"—Marcy sat up—"it's Ulysses—and he's carrying something—I'll let him in."

She was away before Jill could move and the black cat flashed into the room and under Jill's bed as if he feared his find would be taken from him. They could hear him growling softly and both girls hung over the side trying to look, finally rolling off on the floor.

"What you got, cat?" demanded Marcy. "Let's see now—"

But though Ulysses was crouched growling, and he had certainly had something in his mouth when Marcy let him in, there was nothing at all except his own black form now to be seen.

"What did he do with it?"

"I don't know." Marcy was as surprised as Jill. "What was it anyhow?"

But when they compared notes they discovered that neither of them had seen it clearly enough to guess. Jill went for the big flashlight always kept on the table in the hall. She flashed the beam back and forth under, where it shone on Ulysses' sleek person, but showed nothing else at all.

"Got away," Marcy said.

"But if it's in the room somewhere, whatever it is—" Jill did not like the thought of a released something here—especially a something which she could not identify.

"We'll keep Ulysses here. If it comes out, he'll get it. He's just waiting. You shut the door so it can't get out in the hall, and he'll catch it again."

But it was not long before Ulysses apparently gave up all thoughts of hunting and jumped up to sprawl at sleepy ease on the bed. When it came time for Marcy to leave Jill had a plea.

"Marcy, you said Ulysses is half mine, let him stay here tonight. If that—that thing is loose in here, I don't want it on me. Maybe he can catch it again."

"Okay, if he'll stay. Will you, Ulysses?"

He raised his head, yawned and settled back.

"Looks like he chooses so. But if he makes a fuss in the night, you'll have to let him out quick. He yells if you don't—real loud."

Ulysses showed no desire to go out in the early evening. Jill brought in some of his food, which Marcy had delivered, and a tin pie plate full of water. He opened his eyes sleepily, looked at her offering and yawned again. Flashlight in hand, she once more made the rounds of the room, forcing herself to lie on her stomach and look under the bed. But she could see nothing at all. What *had* Ulysses brought in? Or had they been mistaken and only thought he had something?

A little reluctantly Jill crawled into bed, dropping the edge of the sheet over Ulysses. She did not know how Aunt Abby would accept this addition to the household, even if it were temporary, and she did not want to explain. Aunt Abby certainly would not accept with anything but alarm the fact that Ulysses had brought in something and loosed it in Jill's room.

Aunt Abby came and took away the lamp and Ulysses cooperated nicely by not announcing his presence by either voice or movement under the end of sheet. But Jill fought sleep. She had a fear which slowly became real horror, of waking to find *something* perhaps right on her pillow.

Ulysses was stretched beside her. Now he laid one paw across her leg as if he knew exactly how she felt and wanted to reassure her, both of his presence and the fact he was on guard. She began to relax.

She—she was not in bed at all! She was back in a sealed apartment but the breather had failed, she could not breathe— her respirator—the door—she must get out—away where she could breathe! She must! Jill threw herself at the wall. There were no doors—no vents! If she pounded would some one hear?

Then it was dark and she was back in the room, sitting up in bed. A small throaty sound—that was Ulysses. He had moved to the edge of the bed, was crouched there—looking down at the floor. Jill was sweating, shaking with the fear of that dream, it must have been a dream—

But she was awake and still she felt it—that she could hardly breathe, that she must get out—back—back to—

It was as if she could see it right before her like a picture on the wall—the lake—the almost dead lake!

But she did not want—she did—she must—

Thoroughly frightened, Jill rocked back and forth. She did not want to go to the lake, not now. Of course, she didn't! What was the matter with her?

But all she could see was the lake. And, fast conquering her resistance, was the knowledge that she must get up—yes, right now—and go to the lake.

She was crying, so afraid of this thing which had taken over her will, was making her do what she shrank from, that she was shivering uncontrollably as she slid from the bed.

It was then that she saw the eyes!

At first they seemed only pricks of yellow down at floor level, where she had put the pan of water for Ulysses. But when they moved—!

Jill grabbed for the flashlight. Her hands were so slippery with sweat that she almost dropped it. Somehow she got it focused on the pan, pushed the button.

There was something squatting in the pan, slopping the water out on the floor as it flopped back and forth, its movements growing wilder. But save for general outlines—she could hardly see it.

"Breathe—I can't breathe!" Jill's hoarse whisper brought another small growl from Ulysses. But she could breathe, there was no smog here. This was a Clear Outside. What was the matter—?

It was not her—some door in her own mind seemed to open—it was the thing over there flopping in the pan—it couldn't breathe—had to have water—

Jill scuttled for the door, giving the pan and the flopper a wide berth. She laid the flashlight on the floor, slipped around the door and padded towards the kitchen. The cupboard was on the right, that was where she had seen the big kettle when Aunt Abby had talked about canning.

There was moonlight in the kitchen, enough to let her find the cupboard, bring out the kettle. Then—fill it—she worked as noiselessly as she could. Not too full or it would be too heavy for her to carry—

As it was, she slopped water over the edge all the way back to the bedroom. Now—

The floppings in the pan had almost stopped. Jill caught her breath at the feeling inside her—the thing was dying. Fighting her fear and repulsion, Jill somehow got across the room, snatched up the pan before she could let her horror of what it held affect her and tipped all its contents into the kettle. There was an alien touch against her fingers as it splashed in. But—she could hardly see it now!

She knelt by the kettle, took the torch and shone it into the depths.

It—it was like something made of glass! She could see the bulbous eyes, they were solid, and some other parts, but the rest seemed to melt right into the water.

Jill gave a small sound of relief. That compulsion which had held her to the creature's need was lifted. She was free.

She sat back on her heels by the kettle, still shining the torch at the thing. It had flopped about some at first, but now it was settled quietly at the bottom.

A sound out of the dark, Ulysses poked his head over the other side of the kettle to survey its inhabitant. He did not growl, and he stood so for only a moment or two before going to jump back on the bed with the air of one willing to return to sleep now that all the excitement was over.

For a time the thing was all right, Jill decided. She was more puzzled than alarmed now. Her acquaintance with things living Outside was so small, only through reading and what she had learned from Marcy and observation these past days. But how had the thing made her wake up, know what it had to have to live? She could not remember ever having known that things which were not people could think you into doing what they wanted.

When she was very little—the old fairy tale book which had been her mother's—a story about a frog who was really a prince. But that was only a story. Certainly this almost transparent thing would never have been a person!

It came from the lake, she was sure of that from the first

picture in her mind after she woke up. And it wanted to go back there.

Tonight?

Almost as if she had somehow involuntarily asked a question! A kind of urgency swept into her mind in answer. Yes—now—now! It was answering her as truly as if it had come to the surface of the water and shouted back at her.

To go out in the night? Jill cringed. She did not dare, she simply could not. Yet now the thing—it was doing as it had before—pushing her into taking it back.

Jill fought with all the strength of will she had. She could *not* go down to the lake now—

But she was gasping—the thing—it was making her feel again something of what if felt—its earlier agony had been only a little relieved by the bringing of the kettle. It had to be returned to the lake and soon.

Slowly Jill got up and began to dress. She was not even sure she could find the way by night. But the thing would give her no peace. At last, lugging the kettle with one hand, holding the flash in the other, she edged out into the night.

There were so many small sounds—different kinds of bugs maybe, and some birds. Before the bad times there had been animals—before the Cleanup when most everything requiring air men could use had been killed. Maybe—here in the Outside there were animals left.

Better not think of that! Water sloshing over the rim of the kettle at every step, Jill started on the straightest line possible for the lake. When she got behind the first screen of bushes she turned on the flash and found the now familiar way. But she could not run as she wished, she had to go slowly to avoid a fall on this rough ground.

So she reached the bank of the lake. The moon shone so brightly she snapped off the flash. Then she was aware of movement—the edges of the thick banks of vegetation which had grown from the lake bottom to close over the water were in constant motion, a rippling. Portions of leaf and stem were torn away, floating out into the clear patches, where they went into violent agitation and were pulled completely under. But there was no sign of what was doing this.

In—in! The thought was like a shout in her mind. Jill set down the torch, took the kettle in both hands, dumped its contents down the bank.

Then, fully released from the task the thing had laid upon her, she grabbed for the flash and ran for the house, the empty kettle banging against her legs. Nor did her heart stop its pounding until she was back in bed, Ulysses once more warm and heavy along her leg, purring a little when she reached down to smooth his fur.

Marcy had news in the morning.

"Those Williamses are going to try to blow up the lake, they're afraid something poisonous is out there. Beeny is clear out of his head and all the Williamses went into town to get a dynamite permit."

"They—they can't do that!" Though Jill did not understand at first her reason for that swift denial.

Marcy was eyeing her. "What do you know about it?"

Jill told her of the night's adventure.

"Let's go see—right now!" was Marcy's answer.

Then Jill discovered curiosity overran the traces of last night's fear.

"Look at that, just look at that!" Marcy stared at the lake. The stretches of open water were well marked this morning. All that activity last night must have brought this about.

"If those invisible things are cutting out all the weeds," Marcy observed, "then they sure are doing good. It was those old weeds which started a lot of the trouble. Dad says they got in so thick they took out the oxygen and then the fish and things died but the weeds kept right on. Towards the last, some of the men who had big houses on the other side of the lake tried all sorts of things. They even got new kinds of fish they thought would eat the weeds and dumped those in—brought them from Africa and South America and places like that. But it didn't do any good. Most of the fish couldn't live here and just died—and others—I guess there weren't enough of them."

"Invisible fish?" If there was a rational explanation for last night, Jill was only too eager to have it.

Marcy shook her head. "Never heard of any like those. But they'd better make the most of their time. When the Williamses bomb the lake—"

"Bomb it?"

"Use the dynamite—like bombing."

"But they can't!" Jill wanted to scream that loud enough so that the Williamses 'way off in their mucky old house could hear every word. "I'm going to tell Uncle Shaw—right now!"

Marcy trailed behind her to the house. It was going to take almost as much courage to go into Uncle Shaw's forbidden quarters as it did to transport the kettle to the lake. But just as that had to be done, so did this.

She paused outside the kitchen. Aunt Abby was busy there, and if they went in, she would prevent Jill's reaching Uncle Shaw. They had better go around the house to the big window.

To think that was easier than to do so, the bushes were so thick. But Jill persisted with strength she did not know she had until she came to use it. Then she was looking into the long room. There were books, some crowded on shelves, but others in untidy piles on the floor, and a long table with all kinds of things on it.

But in a big chair Uncle Shaw was sitting, just sitting—staring straight at the window. There was no change in his expression, it was as if he did not see Jill.

She leaned forward and rapped on the pane, and his head jerked as if she had awakened him. Then he frowned and motioned her to go away. But Jill did as she would not have dared to do a day earlier, stood her ground, and pointed to the window, made motions to open it.

After a long moment Uncle Shaw got up, moving very slowly as if it were an effort. He came and opened the long window, which had once been a door onto the overgrown patio.

"Go away," he said flatly.

Jill heard a rustle behind her as if Marcy were obeying. But she stood her ground, though her heart was beating fast again.

"You've got to stop them," she said in a rush.

"Stop them—stop who—from doing what?" He talked slowly as he had moved.

"Stop them from bombing the lake. They'll kill all the invisibles—"

Now his eyes really saw her, not just looked at something which was annoying him.

"Jill—Marcy—" he said their names. "What are you talking about?"

"The Williamses, they're going to bomb the lake on account of what happened to Beeny," Jill said as quickly as she could, determined to make him hear this while he seemed to be listening to her. "That'll kill all the invisibles. And they're eating off the weeds—or at least they break them off and pull them out and sink them or something. There's a lot more clear water this morning."

"Clear water?" He came out, breaking a way through the bush before the window. "Show me—and then tell me just what you are talking about."

It was when Uncle Shaw stood on the lake bank and they pointed out the clear water that Jill told of Ulysses' hunting and its results in detail. He stopped her from time to time to make her repeat parts, but she finally came to the end.

"You see—if they bomb the lake—then the invisibles—they'll all be dead!" she ended.

"You say it talked to you—in your mind—" For the third time he returned to that part of her story. She was beginning to be impatient. The important thing was to stop the Williamses, not worry over what happened last night.

"Not talked exactly, it made me feel bad just like it was feeling, just as if I were caught where a breather broke down. It was horrible!"

"Needed water— Yet by your account it had been quite a long time out of it."

She nodded. "Yes, it needed water awfully bad. It was flopping around in the pan I put down for Ulysses. Then I got the kettle for it, but that wasn't enough either—it needed the lake. When I brought it down—there was all that tearing at the weeds—big patches pulled loose and sunk. But if the Williamses—"

He had been looking over her head at the water. Then he turned abruptly. "Come on!" was the curt order he threw at them and they had to trot fast to keep at his heels.

It was Marcy's house they went to, Marcy's Dad she was told to retell her story to. When she had done, Uncle Shaw looked at Major Scholar.

"What do you think, Price?"

"There were those imports Jacques Brazan bought—"

"Something invisible in water, but something which can live out of it for fairly long stretches of time. Something that can 'think' a distress call. That sound like any of Brazan's pets?"

"Come to think of it, no. But what do you have then, Shaw? Nothing of the old native wildlife fits that description either."

"A wild, very wild guess." Uncle Shaw rubbed his hands together. "So wild you might well drag me in with Beeny, so I won't even say it yet. What did Brazan put in?"

"Ought to be in the records." Major Scholar got a notebook

out of his desk. "Here it is—" He ran his finger down a list. "Nothing with any remote resemblance. But remember Arthur Pierce? He went berserk that day and dumped his collection in the lake."

"He had some strange things in that! No listing though—"

"Dad," Marcy spoke up. "I remember Dr. Pierce's big aquarium. There was a fish that walked on its fins out of water, it could jump, too. He showed me once when I was little, just after we came here."

"Mudskipper!" Her father nodded. "Wait—" He went to a big bookcase and started running his finger along under the titles of the books. "Here—now—" He pulled out a book and slapped it open on the desk.

"Mudskipper—but—wait a minute! Listen here, Shaw!" He began to read, skipping a lot. " 'Pigmy goby—colorless except for eyes—practically transparent in water'—No, this is only three-eighths of an inch long—"

"It was a lot bigger," protested Jill. "Too big for the pie pan I had for Ulysses. It flopped all over in that trying to get under the water."

"Mutant—just maybe," Uncle Shaw said. "Which would fit in with that idea of mine." But he did not continue to explain, saying instead:

"Tonight, Price, we're going fishing!"

He was almost a different person, Jill decided. Just as if the Uncle Shaw she had known since she arrived had been asleep and was now fully awake.

"But the Williamses are going to bomb—" she reminded him.

"Not now—at least not yet. This is important enough to pull a few strings, Price. Do you think we can still pull them?"

Major Scholar laughed. "One can always try, Shaw. I'm laying the smart money all on you."

After dark they gathered at the lake edge. Uncle Shaw and Major Scholar had not said Jill and Marcy could not go too, so they were very much there, and also Aunt Abby and Mrs. Scholar.

But along the beds of vegetation there was no whirling tonight. Had—had she dreamed it, Jill began to wonder apprehensively. And what would Uncle Shaw, Major Scholar, say when no invisibles came?

Then—just as it had shot into her mind last night from the despairing captive in the pan—she knew!

"They won't come," she said with conviction. "Because they know that you have that—that you want to *catch* them!" She pointed to the net, the big kettle of water they had waiting. "They are afraid to come!"

"How do they know?" Uncle Shaw asked quietly. He did not say he didn't believe her, as she expected him to.

"They—somehow they know when there's danger."

"All right." He had been kneeling on the bank, now he stood up. But he stooped again and threw the net behind him, kicked out and sent the water cascading out of the kettle. "We're not going to try to take them."

"But—" Major Scholar began to protest and then said in another tone, "I see—see what you mean—we reacted in the old way—making the same old mistake."

They were all standing now and the moon was beginning to silver the lake. Suddenly there was movement along the edge of the beds, the water rippled, churned. The invisibles were back.

Uncle Shaw held out his hands. One of them caught Jill's in a warm grip, with the other he held Aunt Abby's.

"I think, Price, perhaps—just perhaps we have been given another chance. If we can step out of the old ways enough to take it—no more mistakes—"

"Perhaps so, Shaw."

"You won't let the Williamses—" began Jill.

"No!" That word was as sharp and clear as a shout. It even seemed to echo over the moon-drenched water, where there was that abundant rippling life. "Not now, not ever—I promise you that!" But Jill thought he was not answering her but what was in the water.

"The moon is very bright tonight—" Aunt Abby spoke a little hesitatingly.

"Perhaps it calls to its own. Pierce's creatures may have provided the seed, but remember," Uncle Shaw said slowly, "there was something else down there—"

"Those moon rocks!" Marcy cried.

"Shaw, surely you don't think—!" Major Scholar sounded incredulous.

"Price, I'm not going to think right now, the time has come to accept. If Wilson's suspicions were the truth and those bits of rock from the last pickup had some germ of life locked into them—a germ which reacted on this—then think, man, what the rest of the lunar harvest might mean to this world now!"

"And we know just where—"

Uncle Shaw laughed. "Yes, Price. Since they are now dusty and largely forgotten why shouldn't we make a little intelligent use of them right here. Then watch what happens in a world we befouled! It could be our answer is right up there and we were too blind to see it!"

On the lake the moonlight was shivered into a thousand fragments where the invisibles were at work.

THE LONG NIGHT
OF WAITING

W hat—what are we going to do?" Lesley squeezed her hands so tightly together they hurt. She really wanted to run as far and as fast as she could.

Rick was not running. He stood there, still holding Alex's belt, just as he had grabbed his brother to keep him from following Matt. Following him where?

"We won't do anything," Rick answered slowly.

"But people'll ask—all kinds of questions. You only have to look at that—" Lesley pointed with her chin to what was now before them.

Alex still struggled for freedom. "Want Matt!" he yelled at the top of his voice. He wriggled around to beat at Rick with his fists.

"Let me go! Let me go—with Matt!"

Rick shook him. "Now listen here, shrimp, Matt's gone. You can't get to him now. Use some sense—look there. Do you see Matt? Well, do you?"

Lesley wondered how Rick could be so calm—accepting all of this just as if it happened every day—like going to school, or watching a tel-cast, or the regular, safe things. How could he just stand there and talk to Alex as if he were grown up and Alex was just being pesty as he was sometimes? She watched Rick wonderingly, and tried not to think of what had just happened.

"Matt?" Alex had stopped fighting. His voice sounded as if he were going to start bawling in a minute or two. And when Alex cried—! He would keep on and on, and they would have questions to answer. If they told the real truth—Lesley drew a deep breath and shivered.

No one, no one in the whole world would ever believe them! Not even if they saw what was right out here in this field now. No one would believe—they would say that she, Lesley, and Rick, and Alex were all mixed up in their minds. And they might even be sent away to a hospital or something! No, they could never tell the truth! But Alex, he would blurt out the whole thing if anyone asked a question about Matt. What could they do about Alex?

Her eyes questioned Rick over Alex's head. He was still

holding their young brother, but Alex had turned, was gripping Rick's waist, looking up at him demandingly, waiting, Lesley knew, for Rick to explain as he had successfully most times in Alex's life. And if Rick couldn't explain this time?

Rick hunkered down on the ground, his hands now on Alex's shoulders.

"Listen, shrimp, Matt's gone. Lesley goes, I go to school—"

Alex sniffed. "But the bus comes then, and you get on while I watch—then you come home again—" His small face cleared. "Then Matt—he'll come back? He's gone to school? But this is Saturday! You an' Lesley don't go on Saturday. How come Matt does? An' where's the bus? There's nothin' but that mean old dozer that's chewin' up things. An' now all these vines and stuff—and the dozer tipped right over an'—" He screwed around a little in Rick's grip to stare over his brother's hunched shoulder at the disaster area beyond.

"No," Rick was firm. "Matt's not gone to school. He's gone home—to his own place. You remember back at Christmas time, Alex, when Peter came with Aunt Fran and Uncle Porter? He came for a visit. Matt came with Lizzy for a visit—now he's gone back home—just like Peter did."

"But Matt said—he said *this* was his home!" countered Alex. "He didn't live in Cleveland like Peter."

"It was his home once," Rick continued still in that grown-up way. "Just like Jimmy Rice used to live down the street in the red house. When Jimmy's Dad got moved by his company, Jimmy went clear out to St. Louis to live."

"But Matt was sure! He said *this* was his home!" Alex

frowned. "He said it over and over, that he had come home again."

"At first he did," Rick agreed. "But later, you know that, Matt was not so sure, was he now? You think about that, shrimp."

Alex was still frowning. At least he was not screaming as Lesley feared he would be. Rick, she was suddenly very proud and a little in awe of Rick. How had he known how to keep Alex from going into one of his tantrums?

"Matt—he did say funny things. An' he was afraid of cars. Why was he afraid of cars, Rick?"

"Because where he lives they don't have cars."

Alex's surprise was open. "Then how do they go to the store? An' to Sunday School, an' school, an' every place?"

"They have other ways, Alex. Yes, Matt was afraid of a lot of things, he knew that this was not his home, that he had to go back."

"But—I want him—he—" Alex began to cry, not with the loud screaming Lesley had feared, but in a way now which made her hurt a little inside as she watched him butt his head against Rick's shoulder, making no effort to smear away the tears as they wet his dirty cheeks.

"Sure you want him," Rick answered. "But Matt—he was afraid, he was not very happy here, now was he, shrimp?"

"With me, he was. We had a lot of fun, we did!"

"But Matt wouldn't go in the house, remember? Remember what happened when the lights went on?"

"Matt ran an' hid. An' Lizzy, she kept telling him an' telling him they had to go back. Maybe if Lizzy hadn't all the time told him that—"

Lesley thought about Lizzy. Matt was little—he was not more than Alex's age—not really, in spite of what the stone said. But Lizzy had been older and quicker to understand. It had been Lizzy who had asked most of the questions and then been sick (truly sick to her stomach) when Lesley and Rick answered them. Lizzy had been sure of what had happened then—just like she was sure about the other—that the stone must never be moved, nor that place covered over to trap anybody else. So that nobody would fall through—

Fall through into what? Lesley tried to remember all the bits and pieces Lizzy and Matt had told about where they had been for a hundred and ten years—a *hundred* and *ten* just like the stone said.

She and Rick had found the stone when Alex had run away. They had often had to hunt Alex like that. Ever since he learned to open the Safe-tee gate he would go off about once a week or so. It was about two months after they moved here, before all the new houses had been built and the big apartments at the end of the street. This was all more like real country then. Now it was different, spoiled—just this one open place left and that (unless Lizzy was right in thinking she'd stopped it all) would not be open long. The men had started to clear it off with the bulldozer the day before yesterday. All the ground on that side was raw and cut up, the trees and bushes had been smashed and dug out.

There had been part of an old orchard there, and a big old

lilac bush. Last spring it had been so pretty. Of course, the apples were all little and hard, and had worms in them. But it had been pretty and a swell place to play. Rick and Jim Bowers had a house up in the biggest tree. Their sign said "No girls allowed," but Lesley had sneaked up once when they were playing Little League ball and had seen it all.

Then there was the stone. That was kind of scary. Yet they had kept going to look at it every once in a while, just to wonder.

Alex had found it first that day he ran away. There were a lot of bushes hiding it and tall grass. Lesley felt her eyes drawn in that direction now. It *was* still there. Though you have to mostly guess about that, only one teeny bit of it showed through all those leaves and things.

And when they had found Alex he had been working with a piece of stick, scratching at the words carved there which were all filled up with moss and dirt. He had been so busy and excited he had not tried to dodge them as he usually did, instead he wanted to know if those were real words, and then demanded that Rick read them to him.

Now Lesley's lips silently shaped what was carved there.

> *A long night of waiting.*
> *To the Memory of our dear children,*
> *Lizzy and Matthew Mendal,*
> *Who disappeared on this spot*
> *June 23, 1861.*

May the Good Lord return them
to their loving parents and this
world in His Own reckoned time.
Erected to mark our years of watching,
June 23, 1900.

It had sounded so queer. At first Lesley had thought it was a grave and had been a little frightened. But Rick had pointed out that the words did not read like those on the stones in the cemetery where they went on Memorial Day with flowers for Grandma and Grandpa Targ. It was different because it never said "dead" but "disappeared."

Rick had been excited, said it sounded like a mystery. He had begun to ask around, but none of the neighbors knew anything—except this had all once been a farm. Almost all the houses on the street were built on that land. They had the oldest house of all. Dad said it had once been the farm house, only people had changed it and added parts like bathrooms.

Lizzy and Matt—

Rick had gone to the library and asked questions, too. Miss Adams, she got interested when Rick kept on wanting to know what this was like a hundred years ago (though of course he did not mention the stone, that was their own secret, somehow from the first they knew they must keep quiet about that). Miss Adams had shown Rick how they kept the old newspapers on film tapes. And when he did his big project for social studies, he had chosen the farm's history, which gave him a good chance to use those films to look things up.

That was how he learned all there was to know about Lizzy and Matt. There had been a lot in the old paper about them. Lizzy Mendal, Matthew Mendal, aged eleven and five—Lesley could almost repeat it word for word she had read Rick's copied notes so often. They had been walking across this field, carrying lunch to their father who was ploughing. He had been standing by a fence talking to Doctor Levi Morris who was driving by. They had both looked up to see Lizzy and Matthew coming and had waved to them. Lizzy waved back and then—she and Matthew— they were just gone! Right out of the middle of an open field they were gone!

Mr. Mendal and the Doctor, they had been so surprised they couldn't believe their eyes, but they had hunted and hunted. And the men from other farms had come to hunt too. But no one ever saw the children again.

Only about a year later, Mrs. Mendal (she had kept coming to stand here in the field, always hoping, Lesley guessed, they might come back as they had gone) came running home all excited to say she heard Matt's voice, and he had been calling "Ma! Ma!".

She got Mr. Mendal to go back with her. And he heard it too, when he listened, but it was very faint. Just like someone a long way off calling "Ma!". Then it was gone and they never heard it again.

It was all in the papers Rick found, the story of how they hunted for the children and later on about Mrs. Mendal hearing Matt. But nobody ever was able to explain what had happened.

So all that was left was the stone and a big mystery. Rick started hunting around in the library, even after he finished his report, and found a book with other stories about people who disappeared. It was written by a man named Charles Fort. Some of it had been hard reading, but Rick and Lesley had both found the parts which were like what happened to Lizzy and Matt. And in all those other disappearances there had been no answers to what had happened, and nobody came back.

Until Lizzy and Matt. But suppose she and Rick and Alex told people now, would any believe them? And what good would it do, anyway? Unless Lizzy was right and people should know so they would not be caught. Suppose someone built a house right over where the stone stood, and suppose some day a little boy like Alex, or a girl like Lesley, or even a mom or dad, disappeared? She and Rick, maybe they ought to talk and keep on talking until someone believed them, believed them enough to make sure such a house was never going to be built, and this place was made safe.

"Matt—he kept sayin' he wanted his mom," Alex's voice cut through her thoughts. "Rick, where was his mom that she lost him that way?"

Rick, for the first time, looked helpless. How could you make Alex understand?

Lesley stood up. She still felt quite shaky and a little sick from the left-over part of her fright. But the worst was past now, she had to be as tough as Rick or he'd say that was just like a girl.

"Alex," she was able to say that quite naturally, and her voice did not sound too queer, "Matt, maybe he'll find his mom now, he was just looking in the wrong place. She's not here any more. You remember last Christmas when you went with Mom to see Santy Claus at the store and you got lost? You were hunting mom and she was hunting you, and at first you were looking in the wrong places. But you did find each other. Well, Matt's mom will find him all right."

She thought that Alex wanted to believe her. He had not pushed away from Rick entirely, but he looked as if he was listening carefully to every word she said.

"You're sure?" he asked doubtfully. "Matt—he was scared he'd never find his mom. He said he kept calling an' calling an' she never came."

"She'll come, moms always do." Lesley tried to make that sound true. "And Lizzy will help. Lizzy," Lesley hesitated, trying to choose the right words, "Lizzy's very good at getting things done."

She looked beyond to the evidence of Lizzy's getting things done and her wonder grew. At first, just after it had happened, she had been so shocked and afraid, she had not really understood what Lizzy had done before she and Matt had gone again. What—what *had* Lizzy learned during that time when she had been in the other place? And how had she learned it? She had never answered all their questions as if she was not able to tell them what lay on the other side of that door, or whatever it was which was between *here* and *there*.

Lizzy's work was hard to believe, even when you saw it right before your eyes.

The bulldozer and the other machines which had been parked there to begin work again Monday morning—Well, the bulldozer was lying over on its side, just as if it were a toy Alex had picked up and thrown as he did sometimes when he got over-tired and cross. And the other machines—they were all pushed over, some even broken! Then there were the growing things. Lizzy had rammed her hands into the pockets of her dress-like apron and brought them out with seeds trickling between her fingers. And she had just thrown those seeds here and there, all over the place.

It took a long time for plants to grow—weeks—Lesley knew. But look—these were growing right while you watched. They had already made a thick mat over every piece of the machinery they had reached, like they had to cover it from sight quickly. And there were flowers opening —and butterflies—Lesley had never seen so many butterflies as were gathering about those flowers, arriving right out of nowhere.

"Rick—how—?" She could not put her wonder into a

full question, she could only gesture toward what was happening there.

Her brother shrugged. It was as if he did not want to look at what was happening. Instead he spoke to both of them sharply.

"Listen, shrimp, Les, it's getting late. Mom and Dad will be home soon. We'd better get there before they do. Remember, we left all the things Matt and Lizzy used out in the summer house. Dad's going to work on the lawn this afternoon. He'll want to get the mower out of there. If he sees what we left there he'll ask questions for sure and we might have to talk. Not that it would do any good."

Rick was right. Lesley looked around her regretfully now. She was not frightened any more—she, well, she would like to just stay awhile and watch. But she reached for Alex's sticky hand. To her surprise he did not object or jerk away, he was still hiccuping a little as he did after he cried. She was thankful Rick had been able to manage him so well.

They scraped through their own private hole in the fence into the backyard, heading to the summer house which Rick and Dad had fixed up into a rainy day place to play and a storage for the outside tools. The camping bags were there, even the plates and cups. Those were still smeared with jelly and peanut butter. Just think, Matt had never tasted jelly and peanut butter before, he said. But he had liked it a lot. Lesley had better sneak those in and give them a good washing. And the milk—Lizzy could not understand how you got milk from a bottle a man brought to your house and not straight from a cow. She seemed almost afraid to drink it. And she had not liked Coke at all—said it tasted funny.

"I wish Matt was here." Alex stood looking down at the sleeping bag, his face clouding up again. "Matt was fun—"

"Sure he was. Here, shrimp, you catch ahold of that and help me carry this back. We've got to get it into the camper before Dad comes."

"Why?"

Oh, dear, was Alex going to have one of his stubborn question-everything times? Lesley had put the plates and cups back into the big paper bag in which she had smuggled the food from the kitchen this morning, and was folding up the extra cover from Matt's bed.

"You just come along and I'll tell you, shrimp," she heard Rick say. Rick was just *wonderful* today. Though Mom always said that Rick could manage Alex better than anyone else in the whole family when he wanted to make the effort.

There, she gave a searching look around as the boys left (one of the bags between them) this was cleared. They would take the other bag, and she would do the dishes. Then Dad could walk right in and never know that Lizzy and Matt had been here for two nights and a day.

Two nights and a day—Lizzy had kept herself and Matt out of sight yesterday when Lesley and Rick had been at school. She would not go near the house, nor let Matt later when Alex wanted him to go and see the train Dad and Rick had set up in the family room. All she had wanted were newspapers. Lesley had taken those to her and some of the magazines Mom had collected for the Salvation Army. She must have read a lot, because when they met her after school, she had a million questions to ask.

It was then that she said she and Matt had to go away, back to where they had come from, that they could not stay in this mixed up horrible world which was not the right one at all! Rick told her about the words on the stones and how long it had been. First she called him a liar and said that was not true. So after dark he had taken a flashlight and went back to show her the stone and the words.

She had been the one to cry then. But she did not for long. She got to asking what was going to happen in the field, looking at the machines. When Rick told her, Lizzy had said quick and hot, no, they mustn't do that, it was dangerous—a lot of others might go through. And *they,* those in the other world, didn't want people who did bad things to spoil everything.

When Rick brought her back she was mad, not at him, but at everything else. She made him walk her down to the place from which you could see the inter-city thru-way, with all the cars going whizz. Rick said he was sure she was scared. She was shaking, and she held onto his hand so hard it hurt. But she made herself watch. Then, when they came back, she said Matt and she—they had to go. And she offered to take Alex, Lesley, and Rick with them. She said they couldn't want to go on living *here.*

That was the only time she talked much of what it was like *there.* Birds and flowers, no noise or cars rushing about nor bulldozers tearing the ground up, everything pretty. It was Lesley who had asked then:

"If it was all that wonderful, why did you want to come back?"

Then she was sorry she had asked because Lizzy's face looked like she was hurting inside when she answered:

"There was Ma and Pa. Matt, he's little, he misses Ma bad at times. Those *others*, they got their own way of life, and it ain't much like ours. So, we've kept a-tryin' to get back. I brought somethin'—just for Ma." She showed them two bags of big silvery leaves pinned together with long thorns. Inside each were seeds, all mixed up big and little together.

"Things grow *there*," she nodded toward the field, "they grow strange-like. Faster than seeds hereabouts. You put one of these," she ran her finger tip in among the seeds, shifting them back and forth, "in the ground, and you can see it grow. Honest-Injun-cross-my-heart-an'-hope-to-die if that ain't so. Ma, she hankers for flowers, loves 'em truly. So I brought her some. Only, Ma, she ain't here. Funny thing— *those* over *there*, they have a feelin' about these here flowers and plants. *They* tell you right out that as long as *they* have these growin' around *they*'re safe."

"Safe from what?" Rick wanted to know.

"I dunno—safe from somethin' as *they* think may change 'em. See, we ain't the onlyest ones gittin' through to *there*. There's others, we've met a couple. Susan—she's older'n me and she dresses funny, like one of the real old time ladies in a book picture. And there's Jim—he spends most of his time off in the woods, don't see him much. Susan's real nice. She took us to stay with her when we got *there*. But she's married to one of *them,* so we didn't feel comfortable most of the time. Anyway *they* had some rules—they asked us right away did we have anything made of iron. Iron is bad for *them, they* can't hold it, it burns *them* bad. And *they* told us right out that if we stayed long we'd change. We ate *their* food and drank *their* drink stuff—that's like cider and it tastes good. That changes people from here. So after awhile anyone who comes through is like *them.* Susan mostly is by now, I guess. When you're changed you don't want to come back."

"But you didn't change," Lesley pointed out. "You came back."

"And how come you didn't change?" Rick wanted to know. "You were there long enough—a hundred and ten years!"

"But," Lizzy had beat with her fists on the floor of the summer house then as if she were pounding a drum. "It weren't that long, it couldn't be! Me, I counted every day! It's only been ten of 'em, with us hunting the place to come through on every one of 'em, calling for Ma and Pa to come and get us. It weren't no hundred and ten years—"

And she had cried again in such a way as to make Lesley's throat ache. A moment later she had been bawling right along with Lizzy. For once Rick did not look at her as if he were disgusted, but instead as if he were sorry, for Lizzy, not Lesley, of course.

"It's got to be that time's different in that place," he said thoughtfully. "A lot different. But, Lizzy, it's true, you know—this is 1971, not 1861. We can prove it."

Lizzy wiped her eyes on the hem of her long apron. "Yes, I got to believe. 'Cause what you showed me ain't my world at all. All those cars shootin' along so fast, lights what go on and off when you press a button on the wall—all these houses built over Pa's good farmin' land—what I read today. Yes, I gotta believe it—but it's hard to do that, right hard!"

"And Matt 'n' me, we don't belong here no more, not with all this clatter an' noise an' nasty smelling air like we sniffed down there by that big road. I guess we gotta go back *there*. Leastwise, we know what's there now."

"How can you get back?" Rick wanted to know.

For the first time Lizzy showed a watery smile. "I ain't no dunce, Rick. *They* got rules, like I said. You carry something outta that place and hold on to it, an' it pulls you back, lets you in again. I brought them there seeds for Ma. But I thought maybe Matt an' me—we might want to go visitin' *there*. Susan's been powerful good to us. Well, anyway, I got these too."

She had burrowed deeper in her pocket, under the packets of seeds and brought out two chains of woven grass, tightly braided. Fastened to each was a small arrowhead, a very tiny one, no bigger than Lesley's little fingernail.

Rick held out his hand. "Let's see."

But Lizzy kept them out of his reach.

"Them's no Injun arrowheads, Rick. Them's what *they* use for *their* own doin's. Susan, she calls them 'elf-shots.' Anyway, these here can take us back if we wear 'em. And we will tomorrow, that's when we'll go."

They had tried to find out more about *there,* but Lizzy would not answer most of their questions. Lesley thought she could not for some reason. But she remained firm in her decision that she and Matt would be better off *there* than *here.* Then she had seemed sorry for Lesley and Rick and Alex that they had to stay in such a world, and made the suggestion that they link hands and go through together.

Rick shook his head. "Sorry—no. Mom and Dad—well, we belong here."

Lizzy nodded. "Thought you would say that. But—it's so ugly now, I can't see as how you want to." She cupped the tiny arrowheads in her hand, held them close. "Over *there* it's so pretty. What are you goin' to do here when all the ground is covered up with houses and the air's full of bad smells, an' those cars go rush-rush all day and night too? Looky here—" She reached for one of the magazines. "I'm the best reader in the school house. Miss Jane, she has me up to read out loud when the school board comes visitin'." She did not say that boastfully, but as if it were a truth everyone would know. "An' I've been readin' pieces in here. They've said a lot about how bad things are gittin' for you all—bad air, bad water—too many people—everything like that. Seems like there's no end but bad here. Ain't that so now?"

"We've been studying about it in school," Lesley agreed, "Rick and me, we're on the pick-up can drive next week. Sure we know."

"Well, this ain't happening over *there,* you can bet you! *They* won't let it."

"How do they stop it?" Rick wanted to know.

But once more Lizzy did not answer. She just shook her head and said *they* had their ways. And then she had gone on:

"Me an' Matt, we have to go back. We don't belong here now, and back *there* we do, sorta. At least it's more like what we're used to. We have to go at the same hour as before—noon time—"

"How do you know?" Rick asked.

"There's rules. We were caught at noon then, we go at noon now. Sure you don't want to come with us?"

"Only as far as the field," Rick had answered for them. "It's Saturday, we can work it easy. Mom has a hair appointment in the morning, Dad is going to drive her 'cause he's seeing Mr. Chambers, and they'll do the shopping before they come home. We're supposed to have a picnic in the field, like we always do. Being Saturday the men won't be working there either."

"If you have to go back at noon," Lesley was trying to work something out, "how come you didn't get here at noon? It must have been close to five when we saw you. The school bus had let us off at the corner and Alex had come to meet us—then we saw you—"

"We hid out," Lizzy had said then. "Took a chance on you 'cause you were like us—"

Lesley thought she would never forget that first meeting, seeing the fair haired girl a little taller than she, her hair in two long braids, but such a queer dress on—like a "granny" one, yet different, and over it a big coarse-looking checked apron. Beside her Matt, in a check shirt and funny looking pants, both of them barefooted. They had looked so unhappy and lost. Alex had broken away from Lesley and Rick and had run right over to them to say "Hi" in the friendly way he always did.

Lizzy had been turning her head from side to side as if hunting for something which should be right there before her. And when they had come up she had spoken almost as if she were angry (but Lesley guessed she was really frightened) asking them where the Mendal house was.

If it had not been for the stone and Rick doing all that hunting down of the story behind it, they would not have known what she meant. But Rick had caught on quickly. He had said that they lived in the old Mendal house now, and they had brought Lizzy and Matt along with them. But before they got there they had guessed who Lizzy and Matt were, impossible as it seemed.

Now they were gone again. But Lizzy, what had she done just after she had looped those grass strings around her neck and Matt's and taken his hand? First she had thrown out all those seeds on the ground. And then she had pointed her finger at the bulldozer, and the other machines which were tearing up the rest of the farm she had known.

Lesley, remembering, blinked and shivered. She had expected Lizzy and Matt to disappear, somehow she had never doubted that they would. But she had not foreseen that the bulldozer would flop over at Lizzy's pointing, the other things fly around as if they were being thrown, some of them breaking apart. Then the seeds sprouting, vines and grass, and flowers, and small trees shooting up—just like the time on TV when they speeded up the camera somehow so you actually saw a flower opening up. What had Lizzy learned *there* that she was able to do all that?

Still trying to remember it all, Lesley wiped the dishes. Rick and Alex came in.

"Everything's put away," Rick reported. "And Alex, he understands about not talking about Matt."

"I sure hope so, Rick. But—how did Lizzy do that— make the machines move by just pointing at them? And how can plants grow so quickly?"

"How do I know?" he demanded impatiently. "I didn't see any more than you did. We've only one thing to remember, we keep our mouths shut tight. And we've got to be just as surprised as anyone else when somebody sees what happened there—"

"Maybe they won't see it—maybe not until the men come on Monday," she said hopefully. Monday was a school day, and the bus would take them early. Then she remembered.

"Rick, Alex won't be going to school with us. He'll be here with Mom. What if somebody says something and he talks?"

Rick was frowning. "Yeah, I see what you mean. So— we'll have to discover it ourselves—tomorrow morning. If we're here when people get all excited we can keep Alex quiet. One of us will have to stay with him all the time."

But in the end Alex made his own plans. The light was only grey in Lesley's window when she awoke to find Rick shaking her shoulder.

"What—what's the matter?"

"Keep it low!" he ordered almost fiercely. "Listen, Alex's gone—"

"Gone where?"

"Where do you think? Get some clothes on and come on!"

Gone to *there?* Lesley was cold with fear as she pulled on jeans and a sweat shirt, thrust her feet into shoes. But how could Alex—? Just as Matt and Lizzy had gone the first time. They should not have been afraid of being disbelieved, they should have told Dad and Mom all about it. Now maybe Alex would be gone for a hundred years. No—not Alex!

She scrambled down stairs. Rick stood at the back door waving her on. Together they raced across the backyard, struggled through the fence gap and—

The raw scars left by the bulldozer were gone. Rich foliage

rustled in the early morning breeze. And the birds—! Lesley had never seen so many different kinds of birds in her whole life. They seemed so tame, too, swinging on branches, hopping along the ground, pecking a fruit. Not the sour old apples but golden fruit. It hung from bushes, squashed on the ground from its own ripeness.

And there were flowers—and—

"Alex!" Rick almost shouted.

There he was. Not gone, sucked into *there* where they could never find him again. No he was sitting under a bush where white flowers bloomed. His face was smeared with juice as he ate one of the fruit. And he was patting a bunny! A real live bunny was in his lap. Now and then he held fruit for the bunny to take a bite too. His face, under the smear of juice, was one big smile. Alex's happy face which he had not worn since Matt left.

"It's real good," he told them.

Scrambling to his feet he would have made for the fruit bush but Lesley swooped to catch him in a big hug.

"You're safe, Alex!"

"Silly!" He squirmed in her hold. "Silly Les. This is a good place now. See, the bunny came 'cause he knows that. An' all the birds. This is a *good* place. Here—" he struggled out of her arms, went to the bush and pulled off two of the fruit. "You eat—you'll like them."

"He shouldn't be eating those. How do we know it's good for him?" Rick pushed by to take the fruit from his brother.

Alex readily gave him one, thrust the other at Lesley.

"Eat it! It's better'n anything!"

As if she had to obey him, Lesley raised the smooth yellow fruit to her mouth. It smelled—it smelled good—like everything she liked. She bit into it.

And the taste—it did not have the sweetness of an orange, nor was it like an apple or a plum. It wasn't like anything she had eaten before. But Alex was right, it was good. And she saw that Rick was eating, too.

When he had finished her elder brother turned to the bush and picked one, two, three, four—

"You *are* hungry," Lesley commented. She herself had taken a second. She broke it in two, dropped half to the ground for two birds. Their being there, right by her feet, did not seem in the least strange. Of course one shared. It did not matter if life wore feathers, fur, or plain skin, one shared.

"For Mom and Dad," Rick said. Then he looked around.

They could not see the whole of the field, the growth was too thick. And it was reaching out to the boundaries. Even as Lesley looked up a vine fell like a hand on their own fence, caught fast, and she was sure that was only the beginning.

"I was thinking Les," Rick said slowly. "Do you remember what Lizzy said about the fruit from *there* changing people? Do you feel any different?"

"Why no." She held out her finger. A bird fluttered up to perch there, watching her with shining beads of eyes. She laughed. "No, I don't feel any different."

Rick looked puzzled. "I never saw a bird that tame before.

Well, I wonder—Come on, let's take these to Mom and Dad."

They started for the fence where two green runners now clung. Lesley looked at the house, down the street to where the apartment made a monstrous outline against the morning sky.

"Rick, why do people want to live in such ugly places. And it smells bad—"

He nodded. "But all that's going to change. You know it, don't you?"

She gave a sigh of relief. Of course she knew it. The change was beginning and it would go on and on until *here* was like *there* and the rule of iron was broken for all time.

The rule of iron? Lesley shook her head as if to shake away a puzzling thought. But, of course, she must have always known this. Why did she have one small memory that this was strange? The rule of iron was gone, the long night of waiting over now.

THROUGH THE NEEDLE'S EYE

I t was not her strange reputation which attracted me to old Miss Ruthevan, though there were stories to excite a solitary child's morbid taste. Rather it was what she was able to create, opening a whole new world to the crippled girl I was thirty years ago.

Two years before I made that momentous visit to Cousin Althea I suffered an attack of what was then known as infantile paralysis. In those days, before Salk, there was no cure. I was fourteen when I met Miss Ruthevan, and I had been told for weary months that I was lucky to be able to walk at all, even though I must do so with a heavy brace on my right leg. I might accept that verdict outwardly, but the me imprisoned in the thin adolescent's body was a rebel.

Cousin Althea's house was small, and on the wrong side of the wrong street to claim gentility. (Cramwell did not have a railroad to separate the comfortable, smug sheep from the aspiring goats.) But her straggling back garden ran to a wall of mellow, red brick patterned by green moss, and in one place a section of this barrier had broken down so one could hitch up to look into the tangled mat of vine and brier which now covered most of the Ruthevan domain.

Three-fourths of that garden had reverted to the wild, but around the bulk of the house it was kept in some order. The fat, totally deaf old woman who ruled Miss Ruthevan's domestic concerns could often be seen poking about, snipping off flowers or leaves after examining each with the care of a cautious shopper, or filling a pan with wizened berries. Birds loved the Ruthevan garden and built whole colonies of nests in its unpruned trees. Bees and butterflies were thick in the undisturbed peace. Though I longed to explore, I never quite dared, until the day of the quilt.

That had been a day of disappointment. There was a Sunday school picnic to which Ruth, Cousin Althea's daughter, and I were invited. I knew that it was not for one unable to play ball, race or swim. Proudly I refused to go, giving the mendacious excuse that my leg ached. Filled with bitter envy, I watched Ruth leave. I refused Cousin Althea's offer to let me make candy, marching off, lurch-push to perch on the wall.

There was something new in the garden beyond. An expanse of color flapped languidly from a clothes line, giving tantalizing glimpses of it. Before I knew it, I tumbled over the wall, acquiring a goodly number of scrapes and bruises on the way, and struggled through a straggle of briers to see better.

It was worth my struggle. Cousin Althea had quilts in plenty, mostly made by Grandma Moss, who was considered by the family to be an artist at needlework. But what I viewed now was as clearly above the best efforts of Grandma as a Rembrandt above an inn sign.

This was appliqué work, each block of a different pattern; though, after some study, I became aware that the whole was to be a panorama of autumn. There were flowers, fruits, berries, and nuts, each with their attendant clusters of leaves, while the border was an interwoven wreath of maple and oak foliage in the richest coloring. Not only was the appliqué so perfect one could not detect a single stitch, but the quilting over-pattern was as delicate as lace. It was old; its once white background had been time-dyed cream; and it was the most beautiful thing I had ever seen.

"Well, what do you think of it?"

I lurched as I tried to turn quickly, catching for support at the trunk of a gnarled apple tree. On the brick wall from the house stood old Miss Ruthevan. She was tall and held herself stiffly straight, the masses of her thick, white hair built into a formal coil which, by rights, should have supported a tiara. From throat to instep she was covered by a loose robe in a neutral shade of blue-gray which fully concealed her body.

Ruth had reported Miss Ruthevan to be a terrifying person; her nickname among the children was "old witch." But after my first flash of panic, I was not alarmed, being too bemused by the quilt.

"I think it's wonderful. All fall things—"

"It's a bride quilt," she replied shortly, "made for a September bride."

She moved and lost all her majesty of person, for she limped in an even more ungainly fashion than I, weaving from side to side as if about to lose her balance at any moment. When she halted and put her hand on the quilt, she was once more an uncrowned queen. Her face was paper white, her lips blue lines. But her sunken, very alive eyes probed me.

"Who are you?"

"Ernestine Williams. I'm staying with Cousin Althea." I pointed to the wall.

Her thin brows, as white as her hair, drew into a small frown. Then she nodded. "Catherine Moss's granddaughter, yes. Do you sew, Ernestine?"

I shook my head, oddly ashamed. There was a vast importance to that question, I felt. Maybe that gave me the courage to add, "I wish I could—like that." I pointed a finger at the quilt. I surprised myself, for never before had I wished to use a needle.

Miss Ruthevan's clawlike hand fell heavily on my shoulder. She swung her body around awkwardly, using me as a pivot, and then drew me along with her. I strove to match my limp to her wider lurch, up three worn steps into a hallway, which was very dark and cool out of the sun.

Shut doors flanked us, but the one at the far end stood open, and there she brought me, still captive in her strong grasp. Once we were inside she released me, to make her own crab's way to a tall-backed chair standing in the full light of a side window. There she sat enthroned, as was right and proper.

An embroidery frame stood before the chair, covered with a throw of white cloth. At her right hand was a low table bearing a rack of innumerable small spindles, each wound with colorful thread.

"Look around," she commanded. "You are a Moss. Catherine Moss had some skill; maybe you have inherited it."

I was ready to disclaim any of my grandmother's talent; but Miss Ruthevan, drawing off the shield cloth and folding it with small flicks, ignored me. So I began to edge nervously about the room, staring wide-eyed at the display there.

The walls were covered with framed, glass-protected needlework. Those pieces to my left were very old, the colors long faded, the exquisite stitchery almost too dim to see. But, as I made my slow progress, each succeeding picture became brighter and more distinct. Some were the conventional samplers, but the majority were portraits or true pictures. As I skirted needlework chairs and dodged a fire screen, I saw that the art was in use everywhere. I was in a shrine to needle creations which had been brought to the highest peak of perfection and beauty. As I made that journey of discovery, Miss Ruthevan stitched away the minutes, pausing now and then to study a single half-open white rose in a small vase on her table.

"Did you make all these, Miss Ruthevan?" I blurted out at last.

She took two careful stitches before she answered. "No. There have always been Ruthevan women so talented, for three hundred years. It began"—her blue lips curved in a very small shadow of a smile, though she did not turn her attention from her work—"with Grizel Ruthevan, of a family a king chose to outlaw—which was, perhaps, hardly wise of him." She raised her hand and pointed with the needle she held to the first of the old frames. It seemed to me that a sparkle of sunlight gathered on the needle and lanced through the shadows about the picture she so indicated. "Grizel Ruthevan, aged seventeen— she was the first of us. But there were enough to follow. I am the last."

"You mean your—your ancestors—did all this."

Again she smiled that curious smile. "Not all of them, my dear. Our art requires a certain cast of mind, a talent you may certainly call it. My own aunt, for example, did not have it; and, of course, my mother, not being born a Ruthevan, did not. But my great-aunt Vannessa was very able."

I do not know how it came about, but when I left, I was committed to the study of needlework under Miss Ruthevan's teaching; though she gave me to understand from the first that the perfection I saw about me was not the result of amateur work, and that here, as in all other arts, patience and practice as well as aptitude were needed.

I went home full of the wonders of what I had seen; and when I cut single-mindedly across Ruth's account of her day, she roused to counterattack.

"She's a witch, you know!" She teetered back and forth on the boards of the small front porch. "She makes people disappear; maybe she'll do that to you if you hang around over there."

"Ruthie!" Cousin Althea, her face flushed from baking, stood behind the patched screen. Her daughter was apprehensively quiet as she came out. But I was more interested in what Ruthie had said than any impending scolding.

"Makes people disappear—how?"

"That's an untruth, Ruthie," my cousin said firmly. True to her upbringing, Cousin Althea thought the word "lie" coarse. "Never let me hear you say a thing like that about Miss Ruthevan again. She has had a very sad life—"

"Because she's lame?" I challenged.

Cousin Althea hesitated; truth won over tact. "Partly. You'd never think it to look at her now, but when she was just a little older than you girls she was a real beauty. Why, I remember mother telling about how people would go to their windows just to watch her drive by with her father, the Colonel. He had a team of matched grays and a carriage he'd bought in New York.

"She went away to school, too, Anne Ruthevan did. And that's where she met her sweetheart. He was the older brother of one of her schoolmates."

"But Miss Ruthevan's an old maid!" Ruth protested. "She didn't ever marry."

"No." Cousin Althea sat down in the old, wooden porch

rocker and picked up a palm leaf fan to cool her face, "No, she didn't ever marry. All her good fortune turned bad almost overnight, you might say.

"She and her father went out driving. It was late August and she was planning to be married in September. There was a bad storm came up very sudden. It frightened those grays and they ran away down on the river road. They didn't make the turn there and the carriage was smashed up. The Colonel was killed. Miss Anne—well, for days everybody thought she'd die, too.

"Her sweetheart came up from New York. My mother said he was the handsomest man: tall, with black hair waving down a little over his forehead. He stayed with the Chambers family. Mr. Chambers was Miss Anne's uncle on her mother's side. He tried every day to see Miss Anne, only she would never have him in—she must have known by then—"

"That she was always going to be lame," I said flatly.

Cousin Althea did not look at me when she nodded agreement.

"He went away, finally. But he kept coming back. After a while people guessed what was really going on. It wasn't Miss Anne he was coming to see now; it was her cousin, Rita Chambers.

"By then Miss Anne had found out some other pretty unhappy things. The Colonel had died sudden, and he left his business in a big tangle. By the time someone who knew how got to looking after it most of the money was gone. Here was Miss Anne, brought up to have most of what she had a mind for; and now she had nothing. Losing her sweetheart to Rita and then her money; it changed her. She shut herself away from most folks. She was awful young—only twenty.

"Pretty soon Rita was planning *her* wedding—they were going to be married in August, just about a year after that ride which changed Miss Anne's life. Her fiancé came up from New York a couple of days ahead of time; he was staying at Doc Bernard's. Well, the wedding day came, and Doc was to drive the groom to the church. He waited a good long time and finally went up to his room to hurry him along a little, but he wasn't there. His clothes were all laid out, nice and neat. I remember hearing Mrs. Bernard, she was awfully old then, telling as how it gave her a turn to see the white rose he was to wear in his buttonhole still sitting in a glass of water on the chest of drawers. But he was gone—didn't take his clothes nor nothing—just went. Nobody saw hide nor hair of him afterwards."

"But what could have happened to him, Cousin Althea?" I asked.

"They did some hunting around, but never found anyone who saw him after breakfast that morning. Most people finally decided he was ashamed of it all, that he felt it about Miss Anne. 'Course, that didn't explain why he left his clothes all lying there. Mother always said she thought both Anne and Rita were well rid of him. It was a ten days' wonder all right, but people forgot in time. The Chamberses took Rita away to a watering place for a while; she was pretty peaked. Two years later she married John Ford; he'd always been sweet on her.

Then they moved out west someplace. I heard as how she'd taken a dislike to this whole town and told John she'd say 'yes' to him provided he moved.

"Since then—well, Miss Anne, she began to do a little better. She was able to get out of bed that winter and took to sewing—not making clothes and such, but embroidery. Real important people have bought some of her fancy pictures; I heard tell a couple are even in museums. And you're a very lucky girl, Ernestine, if she'll teach you like you said."

It was not until I was in bed that night, going over my meeting with Miss Ruthevan and Cousin Althea's story, that something gave me a queer start: the thought of that unclaimed white rose.

Most of the time I had spent with Miss Ruthevan she had been at work. But I had never seen the picture she was stitching, only her hands holding the needle dipping in and out, or bringing a thread into the best light as she matched it against the petals of the rose on her table.

That had been a perfect rose; it might have been carved from ivory. Miss Ruthevan had not taken it out of the glass; she had not moved out of her chair when I left. But now I was sure that, when I had looked back from the door, the rose had been gone. Where? It was a puzzle. But, of course, Miss Ruthevan must have done something with it when I went to look at some one of the pictures she had called to my attention.

Cousin Althea was flattered that Miss Ruthevan had shown interest in me; I know my retelling of the comment about Grandma Moss had pleased her greatly. She carefully supervised my dress before my departure for the Ruthevan house the next day, and she would not let me take the shortcut through the garden. I must limp around the block and approach properly through the front door. I did, uncomfortable in the fresh folds of skirt, so ill looking I believed, above the ugliness of the brace.

Today Miss Ruthevan had put aside the covered frame and was busied instead with a delicate length of old lace, matching thread with extra care. It was a repair job for a museum, she told me.

She put me to work helping her with the thread. Texture, color, shading—I must have an eye for all, she told me crisply. She spun some of her thread herself and dyed much of it, using formulas which the Ruthevan women had developed over the years.

So through the days and weeks which followed I found cool refuge in that high-walled room where I was allowed to handle precious fabrics and take some part in her work. I learned to spin on a wheel older than much of the town, and I worked in the small shed-like summer kitchen skimming dye pots and watching Miss Ruthevan measure bark and dried leaves and roots in careful quantities.

It was only rarely that she worked on the piece in the standing frame, which she never allowed me to see. She did not forbid that in words, merely arranged it so that I did not. But from time to time, when she had a perfectly formed fern, a flower, and once in the early morning when a dew-beaded spider web cornered the window without, she would stitch away. I never saw what she did with her models when she had finished. I only knew that when the last stitch was set to her liking, the vase was empty, the web had vanished.

She had a special needle for this work. It was kept in a small brass box, and she made a kind of ceremony of opening the box, holding it tightly to her breast, with her eyes closed; she also took a great while to thread the needle itself, running the thread back and forth through it. But when Miss Ruthevan did not choose to explain, there was that about her which kept one from asking questions.

I learned, slowly and painfully, with pricked fingers and sick frustration each time I saw how far below my goals my finished work was. But there was a great teacher in Miss Ruthevan. She had patience and her criticism inspired instead of blighted. Once I brought her a shell I had found. She turned it over, putting it on her model table. When I came the next day it still lay there, but on a square of fabric, the outline of the shell sketched upon the cloth.

"Select your threads," she told me.

It took me a long time to match and rematch. She examined my choice and made no changes.

"You have the eye. If you can also learn the skill . . ."

I tried to reproduce the shell; but the painful difference between my work and the model exasperated me, until the thread knotted and snarled and I was close to tears. She took it out of my hand.

"You try too hard. You think of the stitches instead of the

whole. It must be done here as well as with your fingers." She touched one of her cool, dry fingers to my forehead.

So I learned patience as well as skill, and as she worked Miss Ruthevan spoke of art and artists, of the days when she had gone out of Cramwell into a world long lost. I went back to Cousin Althea's each afternoon with my head full of far places and the beauty men and women could create. Sometimes she had me leaf through books of prints, or spend afternoons sorting out patterns inscribed on strips of parchment older than my own country.

The change in Miss Ruthevan herself came so slowly during those weeks that I did not note it at first. When she began to refuse commissions, I was not troubled, but rather pleased, for she spent more time with me, only busy with that on the standing frame. I did regret her refusing to embroider a wedding dress; it was so beautiful. It was that denial which made me aware that now she seldom came out of her chair; there were no more mornings with the dye pots.

One day when I came there were no sounds from the kitchen, a curious silence in the house. My uneasiness grew as I entered the workroom to see Miss Ruthevan sitting with folded hands, no needle at work. She turned her head to watch as I limped across the carpet. I spoke the first thing in my mind.

"Miss Applebee's gone." I had never seen much of the deaf housekeeper, but the muted sounds of her presence had always been with us. I missed them now.

"Yes, Lucy is gone. Our time has almost run out. Sit down,

Ernestine. No, do not reach for your work, I have something to say to you."

That sounded a little like a scolding to come. I searched my conscience as she continued.

"Some day very soon now, Ernestine, I too, shall go."

I stared at her, frightened. For the first time I was aware of just how old Miss Ruthevan must be, how skeleton thin were her quiet hands.

She laughed. "Don't grow so big-eyed, child. I have no intention of being coffined, none at all. It is just that I have earned a vacation of sorts, one of my own choosing. Remember this, Ernestine, nothing in this world comes to us unpaid for; and when I speak of pay, I do not talk of money. Things which may be bought with money are the easy things. No, the great desires of our hearts are paid for in other coin; I have paid for what I want most, with fifty years of labor. Now the end is in sight—see for yourself!"

She pushed at the frame so for the first time I could see what it held.

It was a picture, a vivid one. Somehow I felt that I looked through a window to see reality. In the background to the left, tall trees arched, wearing the brilliant livery of fall. In the foreground was a riot of flowers.

Against a flaming oak stood a man, a shaft of light illuminating his high-held, dark head. His thin face was keenly alive and welcoming. His hair waved down a little over his forehead.

Surrounded by the flowers was the figure of a woman. By the grace and slenderness of her body she was young. But her face was still but blank canvas.

I went closer, fascinated by form and color, seeing more details the longer I studied it. There was a rabbit crouched beneath a clump of fern, and at the feet of the girl a cat, eyeing the hunter with the enigmatic scrutiny of its kind. Its striped, gray and black coat was so real I longed to touch—to see if it were truly fur.

"That was Timothy," Miss Ruthevan said suddenly. "I did quite well with him. He was so old, so old and tired. Now he will be forever young."

"But, you haven't done the lady's face," I ventured.

"Not yet, child, but soon now." She suddenly tossed the cover over the frame to hide it all.

"There is this." She picked up the brass needle-case and opened it fully for the first time, to display a strip of threadbare velvet into which were thrust two needles. They were not the ordinary steel ones, such as I had learned to use, but bright yellow slivers of fire in the sun.

"Once," she told me, "there were six of these—now only two. This one is mine. And this," her finger did not quite touch the last, "shall be yours, if you wish, only if you wish, Ernestine. Always remember one pays a price for power. If tomorrow, or the day after, you come and find me gone, you shall also find this box waiting for you. Take it and use the needle if and when you will—but carefully. Grizel Ruthevan bought this box for a very high price indeed. I do not know whether we should bless or curse her. . . ." Her voice trailed away and I knew without any formal dismissal I was to go. But at the door I hesitated, to look back.

Miss Ruthevan had pulled the frame back into working distance before her. As I watched she made a careful selection of thread, set it in the needle's waiting eye. She took one stitch and then another. I went into the dark silence of the hall. Miss Ruthevan was finishing the picture.

I said nothing to Cousin Althea of that curious interview. The next day I went almost secretly into the Ruthevan house by the way I had first entered it, over the garden wall. The silence was even deeper than it had been the afternoon before. There was a curious deadness to it, like the silence of a house left unoccupied. I crept to the workroom; there was no one in the chair by the window. I had not really expected to find her there.

When I reached the chair, something seemed to sap my strength so I sat in it as all those days I had seen her sit. The picture stood in its frame facing me—uncovered. As I had expected, it was complete. The imperiously beautiful face of the lady was there in detail. I recognized those wing brows, though now they were dark, the eyes, the mouth with its shadow smile; recognized them with a shiver. Now I knew where the rose, the fern, the web and all the other models had gone. I also knew, without being told, the meaning of the gold needles and why the maiden in the picture wore Anne Ruthevan's face and the hunter had black hair.

I ran, and I was climbing over the back wall before I was

truly aware of what I did. But weighting down the pocket of my sewing apron was the brass needle-box. I have never opened it. I am not Miss Ruthevan; I have not the determination, nor perhaps the courage, to pay the price such skill demands. With whom—or *what*—Grizel Ruthevan dealt to acquire those needles, I do not like to think at all.

wizards who barely made livings in tumbledown cottages surrounded by unpleasant bogs or found themselves reduced to caves where water dripped unendingly and bats provided a litter they could well do without. Their clents were landsmen who came to get a cure for an ailing cow or for a stumbling horse. Cow—horse—when a man of magic should be rightfully dealing with the fate of dales, raking in treasure from lords, living in a keep properly patrolled at night by things which snuffled at the doors to keep all unhappy visitors within their chambers from dusk to dawn—or the reverse, depending upon the habits of the visitor. Magicians have a very wide range of guests, willing and unwilling.

Wizards have no age, save in wizardry. And to live for long in a bat- and water-haunted cave sours men. Though even in the beginning, wizards are never of a lightsome temperament. A certain acid view of life accompanies the profession.

And Saystrap considered he had been far too long in a cave. It was far past the time when he should have been raised to at least a minor hill keep with a few grisly servitors, if not to the castle of his dreams. There was certainly no treasure in his cave, but he refused to face the fact that there never would be.

The great difficulty was the length of Saystrap's spells—they were a hindrance to his ambition. They worked very well for as much as twenty-four hours—if he expended top effort in their concoction. He was truly a master of some fine effects with those; he was labeled a dismal failure because they did not last.

Finally he accepted his limitations to the point of working out a method whereby a short-lived spell could be put to good account. To do this, he must have an assistant. But, while a magician of note could pick and choose apprentices, a half-failure such as Saystrap had to take what he might find in a very limited labor market.

Not too far from his cave lived a landsman with two sons. The eldest was a credit to his thrifty upbringing, a noble young man who was upright enough to infuriate all his contemporaries in the neighborhood to whom he was constantly cited as an example. He worked from sunrise to early dusk with a will and never spent silver when copper would do—in all ways an irritating youth.

But his brother was as useless a lad as any father wanted to curse out of house and field. With the mowing hardly begun he could be found lying on his back watching clouds—*clouds,* mind you! Put to any task, he either broke the tools by some stupid misuse or ruined what he was supposed to be working on. And he could not even talk plain, but gobbled away in so thick a voice that no decent man could understand him—not that any wanted to.

It was the latter misfortune that attracted Saystrap's attention. A wizard's power lies in spells, and most of these must be chanted aloud in order to get the proper effect—even a short-time effect. An assistant who was as good as dumb—who would not learn a few tag ends of magic and then have the audacity to set up in business for himself—was the best to employ.

So one morning Saystrap arrived via a satisfactory puff of smoke in the middle of the cornfield where the landsman was berating his son for breaking a hoe. The smoke curled very impressively into the sky as Saystrap stepped out of its curtain. And the landsman jumped back a step or two, looking just as amazed as he should.

"Greetings," said Saystrap briskly. He had long ago learned that any long build-up was not for a short-spelled wizard. It was best to forego the supposedly awed mumbles and get right to the point.

But he did not overlook the staging, of course. A pass or two in the air produced two apple trees about shoulder height. And, as an additional nice touch, a small dragon winked into existence and out again before the landsman found his voice. "It is a fair morning for field work," Saystrap continued.

"It was," the landsman returned a bit uncertainly. Magic in the woods or a cave now—that was one thing. But magic right out in the middle of your best cornfield was a different matter. The dragon was gone, and he could not really swear it had been here. But those trees were still standing where they would be a pesky nuisance around which to get the plow. "How—how can I serve you, Master—Master—?"

"Saystrap," supplied the wizard graciously. "I am your near neighbor, Master Ladizwell. Though busy as you have been on your very fruitful land you may not be aware of that."

Master Ladizwell looked from the trees to the wizard. There was a hint of a frown on his face. Wizards, like the lord's taxmen, were too apt to take more than they gave in return. He did not relish the thought of living cheek by jowl, as it were, with one. And he certainly had not invited this meeting.

"No, you have not," said Saystrap answering his thought. This was the time to begin to bear down a little and let the fellow know just whom and what he was dealing with. "I have come now to ask your assistance in a small matter. I need a pair of younger feet, stronger arms, and a stout back to aid me. Now this lad"—for the first time he glanced at the younger son—"has he ever thought of going into service?"

"Him?" The landsman snorted. "Why, what fool would—" Then he stopped in mid-word. If this wizard did not know of his stupid son's uselessness, why tell the family shame abroad? "For what length of service?" he demanded quickly. If a long bond could be agreed upon, he might get the lout out from underfoot and make a profit into the bargain.

"Oh, the usual—a year and a day."

"And his wages, Master Saystrap?"

"Well, now, at this season another pair of knowledgeable hands—" Ladizwell hurriedly kicked at the broken hoe, hoping the wizard had not seen that nor heard his hot words to his son.

"Will this suffice?" Saystrap waved a hand in a grand, wide gesture, and in the field stood a fine horse.

Ladizwell blinked. "Yes, right enough!" he agreed hurriedly and held out his hand. Saystrap slapped his into it, thus binding the bargain.

Then the wizard gestured again and smoke arose to wreathe both him and his newly engaged servant. When that cleared, they had vanished; and Ladizwell went to put a halter on the horse.

At dawn the next day Ladizwell was far from pleased when he went to the stable to inspect his new prize and found a rabbit instead of a horse nibbling the straw in the stall. At least he did not have to feed and clothe that slip-fingered lout for a year and a day, so perhaps he was still better off than he had been yesterday.

Saystrap, back in his cave, was already making use of his new servant. To him Joachim was a tool with neither wit nor will of his own. But the sooner he began to give what aid he could the better. There were brews boiled and drunk—by Joachim. And he had to be led, or pushed and pulled, through patterns drawn in red and black on the rough floor. But in the end Saystrap was satisfied with the preliminaries and went wearily to his hammock, leaving Joachim to huddle on a bed of bracken.

At dawn the wizard was up and busy again. He allowed Joachim a hasty—and to the lad very untasty—meal of dried roots and berries, hurrying him until Joachim was almost choking on the last bite or two. Then they took to the traveling cloud again and emerged from it not too far from the Market Cross of Hill Dallow. That is—there strode out of the cloud a man in a gray wool tunic leading a fine frisky two-year-old colt, as promising an animal as any one would want to lay eye on. And this was sold at the first calling in the horse fair for a bag of silver pieces heavy enough to weight a man's belt in a satisfying manner.

The colt was led home by the buyer and shown off as being an enviable bargain. But when the moon rose, Joachim stole out of the barn, dropping stall and door latch into place behind him. He shambled off to the far side of the pasture where Saystrap waited impatiently.

This was a game they played several times over, always with a good gain thereby. Saystrap treated Joachim well enough, though more as if he were really a horse than any man. And this was a mistake on Saystrap's part. Joachim might seem stupid and be too thick of speech to talk with his fellows, but he was not slow-witted. He learned from all he heard and saw his master do. Deep in him a small spark of ambition flared. There had not been anything about his father's land that had ever brought that spark into being. There, no matter how hard he tried, his brother could outdo him without seeming to put forth any great effort. But this was another world.

Then, by chance, he learned something that even Saystrap did not know: spells were not always wedded to the spoken word.

His master had sent him to gather herbs in a wild country men seldom traveled. But furred and four-footed hunters had their own well-trodden trails.

For all the barrenness of the wild land Joachim was glad enough to be alone in the open. He missed the fields more than he would have believed possible. It seemed a very long time since he had had a chance to lie and watch the slow passing of clouds overhead and to dream of what he might do if he had a magician's treasure now or had been born into a lord's family.

But this day he found himself mulling over Saystrap's doings rather than paying attention to clouds and his one-time dreams. In his mind he repeated the words he had heard the wizard use in spells. By now the change spell, at least, was as familiar to him as his own name. Then he heard a sound and looked around—into the yellow-green eyes of a snow cat. It hissed a challenge, and Joachim knew that here stalked death on four paws. So, he concentrated—without being sure of how or on what.

The snow cat vanished! On the rock crouched a barn rat.

Joachim shivered. He put out his hand to test the reality of what he saw, and the rat scuttled away squealing. Was this by any chance some ploy of Saystrap's, meant to frighten him into his work? But—there was another way of testing. Joachim looked down at his own body. Did he dare? He thought again.

Soft fur, paws with claws—he was a snow cat! Not quite believing, he leaped up to bound along the ridge. Then he stopped beneath a rock spur and thought himself a man again, more than a little frightened at his own act.

Then that fear became pride, the first time in his life he had cause to feel that. He was a wizard! But only in part. One spell alone could not make him a real one. He must learn more and more and at the same time try to keep his secret from Saystrap if he could. Doubts about that gnawed at him all the way back to the cave.

The only trouble was that Saystrap no longer tried other spells. And the few scraps Joachim assembled from his master's absent-minded mutterings were no help at all. Saystrap was concentrating on what he intended to be his greatest coup in shape-changing.

"The harvest fair at Garth Haigis is the chance to make a

good profit," he told Joachim, mainly because he had to tell someone of his cleverness. "We must have something eye-catching to offer. A pity I cannot change you into a coffer of jewels; I could sell you to more than one buyer. Only then, when the spell faded"—he laughed a little, evilly, and poked Joachim in the ribs with his staff-of-office—"you would be too widely scattered between one keep and the next ever to be put together again." He was deep in thought now, running his long forenail back and forth across his teeth.

"I wonder." He eyed Joachim appraisingly. "A cow is bait only for a landsman. And we have dealt too often in horses; there might be someone with a long memory there." He tapped the end of his staff on the rock. "Ah! A trained hunting falcon—one such as brings a gleam of avarice to any lord's eye!"

Joachim was uneasy. True enough, all Saystrap's tricks had always worked smoothly. He had had no trouble freeing himself from barns and stables when the spell lifted. But keeps were better guarded, and it might not be easy to flee out of those. Then he thought of his own secret. He might in the allotted time cease to be Saystrap's falcon, but that did not mean he had to become an easily recognized man.

The fair at Garth Haigis was an important one. Joachim, wearing falcon shape, gazed about eagerly from his perch on Saystrap's saddle horn. Men in booths remarked on the fine bird and asked its price. But the wizard set such a high one that all shook their heads, though one or two went so far as to count the silver in their belt purses.

Before noon a man wearing the Cross-Key badge of Lord Tanheff rode up to Saystrap.

"A fine bird that—fit for a lord's mews. My lord would like to look at it, Master Falconer."

So Saystrap rode behind the servant to an upper field where tents were set up for the comfort of the nobly born. They summoned to them merchants with such wares as they found interesting.

Lord Tanheff was a man of middle years, and he had no son to lift shield after him. But his daughter, the Lady Juluya, sat at his right hand. Since she was a great heiress, she was the center of a goodly gathering of young lords, each striving to win her attention. It was her way to be fair and show no one favor over his fellows.

She was small and thin. Had she not been an heiress, none perhaps would have found her a beauty. But she had a smile that could warm a man's heart (even if he forgot the gold and lands behind it) and eyes that were interested in all they saw. Once Joachim looked upon her, he could not see anything else.

Neither could Saystrap. It suddenly flashed into his mind as a great illuminating truth that there were other ways of gaining a keep than through difficult spells. One such way was marriage. He did not doubt that, could he gain access to the lady, he would win her. Was he not a wizard and so master of such subtleties that these clods sighing around her now could not imagine?

His planned trickery might also be turned to account. For if he sold Joachim to her father and the bird apparently escaped and returned to him, then he could enter the lady's own hall to bring it back. He could use the pretense of the strayed bird to open all doors.

"Father—that falcon! It is a lordly bird," the Lady Juluya cried as she saw Joachim.

He felt the warmth of pride. Though she saw him as a bird, he was admired. Then he lost that pride. If she could see him as he really was, she would speedily turn away.

Lord Tanheff was as pleased as his daughter and quickly struck a bargain with Saystrap. But the wizard whispered into the bird's ear before he placed it on the gloved hand of the lord's falconer, "Return swiftly tonight!"

Joachim, still watching the Lady Juluya, did not really heed that order. For he was wondering why, at the moment of change, he could not wish himself into some new guise that would bring him close to the lady. He did not have long to watch her, however, for the falconer took him to the keep. Joachim stood on a perch in the mews, hooded now and seeing nothing, left in the dark to get the feel of his new home as was the way with a bird in a strange place. He could hear other hawks moving restlessly and, beyond, the noises of the keep. He wondered how Saystrap thought he could get out of this place in man's shape. Had the wizard some magic plan ready to cover that?

Joachim guessed right. The wizard knew that his falcon-turned-man could not leave the mews as easily as a landsman's barn. He did not trust his assistant to have wits enough to work out any reasonable escape. He himself would move cautiously to effect Joachim's release and not allow magic to be suspected, not when he planned to enchant the Lady Juluya. So Saystrap sat down in a copse near the keep to wait moonrise.

At sunset, however, the clouds gathered, and it was plain that no moon would show. Saystrap could not summon moon magic now, but perhaps he could put the coming storm to account. If he could only be sure when Joachim's change would occur, a matter with which he had never concerned himself before. Had it not been for his new plan to win Lady Juluya, the wizard would not have cared what happened to Joachim. Stupid lads could always be found, but a wizard was entitled to keep his own skin safe. Lord Tanheff, if he did suspect spells, would be just the sort to appeal to some major sorcerer for protection. Saystrap, for all his self-esteem, was not blinded to his own peril from an encounter of that kind.

He could not sit still, but paced back and forth, trying to measure time. To be too early would be as fatal as being too late. The cloud-traveling spell could not be held long. If Joachim could not take to its cover at once, Saystrap could not summon it again that night. He bit his thumbnail, cursing the rain now beginning to fall.

At the keep that same rain drove men to take cover indoors. Joachim heard footsteps in the mews and the voices of the falconer and his assistant. His time for change was close. He shifted on the perch, and the bells fastened to his jesses rang. The footsteps were closing in, and the change was now!

Suddenly he was standing on his own two feet, blinking into

the light of a lantern the falconer held. The man's mouth opened for a shout of alarm. Joachim thought his mind spell.

A snow cat crouched snarling. The falconer, with some presence of mind, threw his lantern at that fearsome beast before he took to his heels, Joachim in great bounds behind. But as the shouting falconer broke one way out of the door, Joachim streaked in the other, trying to reach the outer wall.

That wall was far too high to leap over, but he sped up the stairs leading to the narrow defense walk along its top. Men shouted, and a torch was thrown, nearly striking him. Joachim leaped at a guard aiming a spear, knocked the man down, and was over him and on. Just ahead more men were gathering, bending bows. He thought—

There was no cat on the wall—nothing! The men-at-arms hurried forward, thudding spear heads into every patch of shadow. They were unable to believe that the animal had vanished.

"Wizardry! Tell my lord quickly. There is wizardry here!"

Some stayed to patrol by twos and threes, no man wanting to walk alone in the dark with wizardry loose. The storm struck harder; water rushed over the wall. It washed with such force that it swept away a small gold ring no man had seen in that dusk, carrying it along a gutter, tumbling it out and down, to fall to the muddy earth of the inner garden where the Lady Juluya and her maids grew sweet herbs and flowers. There it lay under the drooping branches of a rain-heavy rose bush.

When the Lord Tanheff heard the report of the falconer and

the wall guards, he agreed that it was plain the falcon had been enchanted and was some stroke of wizardry aimed at the keep. He then dispatched one of his heralds to ride night and day to demand help from the nearest reputable sorcerer, one to whom he already paid a retaining fee as insurance against just such happenings. In the meantime he cautioned all to keep within the walls; the gates were not to be opened for any cause until the herald returned.

Saystrap heard the morning rumors at the fair where men now looked suspiciously at their neighbors, bundling their goods away to be on the road again even though the fair was not officially over. With magic loose who knew where it would strike next? Better be safe, if flatter of purse. The lord had sent for a sorcerer—and with magic opposed to magic anything might happen to innocent bystanders. Magic was no respecter of persons.

The wizard did not give up his plan, however, for the Lady Juluya; it was such a good one. Common sense did not even now baffle his hopes. So he lurked in hiding and made this new plan and that, only to be forced to discard each after some study.

The Lady Juluya, walking in her garden, stooped to raise a rain-soaked rose and saw a glint in the mud. Curious, she dug and uncovered a ring that seemed to slip on her finger almost of its own accord.

"Wherever did you come from?" She held her hand into the watery sunshine of the morning, admiring the ring. She was more than a little pleased at her luck in finding it. Since all her maids denied its loss, she finally decided that it must have lain buried for years until the heavy rain washed it free. She would claim it for her own.

Two days passed; and then three. Still the herald did not return. The Lord Tanheff did not permit the keep gates to be opened. The fairground was deserted now. Saystrap, driven to a rough hiding place in the woods, gnawed his nails down to the quick. Only a fanatical stubbornness kept him lurking there.

None in the lady's tower knew that the ring grew loose and slipped from her finger when she took to her bed at night. It became a mouse feasting on crumbs from her table. Joachim realized that this was a highly dangerous game he played. It would be much wiser to assume wings and feathers once more and be out of the castle with three or four good flaps of his wings. Yet he could not bring himself to leave.

The Lady Juluya was courted and flattered much; yet she was a girl of wit and good humor, wise enough to keep her head. She was both kind and courteous. Time and time again Joachim was tempted to take his true form and tell her his story. But she was seldom alone; when she was, he could not bring himself to do it. Who was he? A loutish clod, so stupid and clumsy he could not even work in the fields nor speak plainly. At his mere appearance he was sure she would summon a guard immediately. And talk! He could not tell anything they would understand.

After the first night he did not remain a mouse, but went out onto the balcony and became a man, squatting in the deepest pool of shadow. He thought about speech and how hard it was for him to shape words to sound like those of others. He practiced saying in whispers the strange sounds he had heard Saystrap mumble, tongue twisters though they were. He did not use them for the binding of spells, but merely to listen to his own voice. By daybreak of the third day he was certain, to his great joy, that he did speak more clearly than he ever had before.

In the woods Saystrap had at last fastened upon a plan he thought would get him into the keep. If he could then be private with the lady only for a short space, he was certain that he could bind her to his will and that all would be as he wished. He had seen the herald ride forth and knew that it might not be too long before he would return with aid.

Though the gates were shut, birds flew over the wall. And pigeons made their nests in the towers and along the roofs. On the fourth day Saystrap assumed a feathered form to join them.

They wheeled and circled, cooed, fluttered, peered in windows, preened on balconies and windowsills. In her garden the Lady Juluya shook out grain for them, and Saystrap was quick to take advantage to such a summons, coming to earth before her.

There is this about wizardry: if you have dabbled even the nail tip of one finger in it, then you have gained knowledge beyond that of ordinary men. The ring that was Joachim recognized the pigeon that was Saystrap. At first he thought his master had come seeking him. Then he noted the wizard-pigeon ran a little this way, back that, and so was pacing out a spell pattern about the feet of Lady Juluya.

Joachim did not know what would happen if Saystrap completed that magic, but he feared the worst. So he loosed his grip on the lady's finger and spun out, to land across one of the lines the pigeon's feet were marking so exactly.

Saystrap looked at the ring and knew it. He wanted none of Joachim, though he was shaken at meeting his stupid apprentice in such a guise. One thing, however, at a time. If this spell were now spoiled or hindered, he might not have another chance. He could settle with Joachim later, after accomplishing his purpose. So with a sharp peck of bill, he sent the ring flying.

Joachim spun behind the rose bush. Then he crept forth again—this time a velvet-footed tom cat. He pounced, and the wildly fluttering pigeon was between his jaws.

"Drop it—you cruel thing!" Lady Juluya struck at the cat. Still gripping the pigeon, Joachim dodged and ran into the courtyard.

Then he found he held no pigeon, but a snarling dog twice his size broke from his grip. He leaped away from Saystrap to the top of a barrel and there grew wings, beak, and talons. Once more a falcon, Joachim was able to soar above the leaping, slavering hound so eager to reach him.

There was no dog, but a thing straight out of a nightmare— half scaled, with leathery wings more powerful than Joachim's and a lashing tail with a wicked spiked end. The creature spiraled up after the falcon into the sky.

He could perhaps outfly it if he headed for the open country.

But he sensed that Saystrap was not intent upon herding an unwilling apprentice back to servitude. He was after the Lady Juluya; therefore there must be fight not flight.

From the monster came such a force of gathered power that Joachim weakened. His poor feat of wizardry was feeble opposed to Saystrap's. With a last despairing beat of wings, he landed on the roof of Lady Juluya's tower and found himself sliding down it, once more a man. While above him circled the griffin, seemingly well content to let him fall to his death on the pavement below.

Joachim summoned power for one last thought.

He fell through the air a gray pebble. So small and so dark a thing escaped Saystrap's eyes. The pebble struck the pavement and rolled into a crack.

Saystrap meanwhile turned to bring victory out of defeat. He alighted in the courtyard and seized upon the Lady Juluya to bear her away. The pebble rolled from hiding, and Joachim stood there. Bare-handed, he threw himself at the monster. This time he shouted words clear and loud, the counterspell which returned Saystrap to his own proper form. Grappling with the wizard, he bore him to the ground, trying to gag him with one hand over his mouth so that he might not utter any more spells.

At that moment the herald rode in upon them as they struggled, ringed around (at a safe distance) by such of the keep folk who were not afraid to be caught in the backlash of any spells from the tangle.

Lord Tanheff shouted an order from the door of the hall to

where he had swept his daughter. The herald tossed at the fighters the contents of a box he had brought back with him (price: one ruby, two medium-sized topazes). These caused a burst a light and a clap of thunder. Joachim stumbled out of a puff of smoke, groping his way blindly. A fat black spider sped in the opposite direction, only to be gobbled up by a rooster.

Well pleased now that they had someone reasonably normal in appearance to blame for all the commotion, the men-at-arms seized Joachim. When he tried to use his spell, he found it did not work. Then the Lady Juluya called imperiously:

"Let him alone!" she ordered. "It was he who attacked the monster on my behalf. Let him tell us who and what he is—"

Let him tell, thought Joachim in despair, *but I cannot do that.* He looked at the Lady Juluya and knew that he must at least try. As he ran his tongue over his lips, she prompted him encouragingly, "Tell us first who you are."

"Joachim," he croaked miserably.

"You are a wizard?"

He shook his head. "Never more than a very small part of one, my lady." So eager was he to let her know the truth of it all that he forgot his stumbling tongue and all else but the tale he had to tell. He told it in a flow of words all could understand.

When he was done, she clapped her hands together and cried, "A fine, brave tale. I claim you equal to such acts. Wizard, half-wizard, third or fourth part of a wizard that you may be reckoned, Joachim, I would like to know you better."

He smiled a little timidly. Though he might be finished with wizardry, anyone the Lady Juluya claimed to be a man had a right to pride. Fortune had served him well this time. If he meddled in magic concerns again, it might not continue to do so.

In that he was a wise man—as he later had chance to prove on numerous occasions. Joachim, his foot firmly planted on the road to success in that hour, never turned back nor faltered.

But the rooster had a severe pain in its middle and was forced to let the spider go. How damaged it was by that abrupt meeting with the irony of fate no man knew thereafter, for Saystrap disappeared.

Under the dome, the city was widespread. Kristie had never known anyone who had gone clear to either end where there were supposed to be gates to the Outside. Not even one of the Bigs as tall and brave as her brother Lew had seen the gates. There was too much Inside.

Also, the gates were of no use. Long ago, years and years before Kristie had been born and before all the Olds had died of the fever, the gates had been fastened tight and were to stay that way forever. Everyone said Outside was bad. You could not breathe because of the poisoned air. There was nothing left alive anymore.

Once Outside must have been wonderful! Some of the Bigs said that the story tapes about Outside were all lies. They were sure it was different from what the readers showed. But Lew said that this wasn't true. All had been just as the tapes said, only very long ago, before the dome had been put over the city.

Lew liked reading tapes more than most of the Bigs. When Kristie had been little, he had taken her with him to the teaching center where there were tapes for Littles, too. And Lew had run one of the readers just for her while he watched another.

The story tapes were all made up. Lew had explained carefully to her about the difference between a made-up story and what had once been real but was not now. Sometimes Kristie wondered how Lew could be so sure that Outside was gone. If no one had even tried to find the gates or to look out, then how could one be sure? Kristie had her own ideas about what might be there though she never told anyone.

The Olds had all died with the fever. Lew was nine years old when it happened, and Kristie was just a baby. There were only a few Crowds left now—Lew's and Brad's and a couple more Kristie had heard the Bigs talk about.

Each Crowd had their street of homes and their own looting places. Sometimes they visited. But mostly they kept to their own streets. The wiggle-walks, which used to carry people across the city, did not run anymore. And in some places the breathers had broken down, so there was only stale, bad air.

Kristie knew their street and she knew the way to the teaching center very well. She had gone looting twice with Fanna, Peggy and Lew. They hunted canned food and clothing, which proved that the Bigs thought Kristie was not a real Little anymore.

But what lay beyond their own territory? Kristie was not even sure which way one would go to get to a gate and maybe see Outside. However, just the night before she'd had an idea. Now she sat on the stalled wiggle-walk while she waited for Lew and thought about it.

There were so many tapes in the teaching center. Fanna went there often because she wanted to learn from the tapes how to make sick people well. Lew looked at tapes about how to run old machines and what life used to be like in the city.

Most of the Bigs and Littles of the Crowd did not care much about learning things. They would rather loot or sit around listening to music packs. Lew said they were dummies.

But Kristie was not a dummy. Today she was going to prove it. Somewhere among all the tapes there ought to be one about the city. Perhaps it would show how one could travel from place to place without getting lost. Such a guide must show the gates. If she could learn how to reach one of the gates, then she would go there.

She had to know—she just had to—whether Outside was as Lew said, a place where no one could breathe or live. Or whether it was as the tapes showed—all green, with water running out in the open over the ground. There might be colored flowers, bright as the pieces of cloth the looters found, and furry things—furry things that could be alive!

Kristie could hardly believe the wonder of that, though Lew told her it had once been true. The only furry things alive Inside were rats.

She shivered when she thought of them. Horrid things! The Bigs shot them with stunners whenever they could. But the furry animals on the tapes were not a bit like rats, not in the least.

"Kristie? Ready to go?"

She jumped eagerly to her feet. Lew stood there alone, so she guessed that Fanna was not going today. Lew was growing so tall that, even though he was a Big, he looked like some of the Olds on the tapes. No one could remember just how many birthdays anyone had had. Kristie wasn't even sure she was nine years old, but she did know Lew was a lot older than she.

He had a nice face and he smiled a lot. And the other Bigs listened to him when there was something important to be decided. Lew was the leader of the Crowd, which made him an important person. He wore a stunner and a beam-light on his belt. Today he had on a new shirt, too, which they had found looting. It was red and Kristie thought red was just right for Lew with his dark hair.

Together they went along the wiggle-walk. Kristie could just remember when it was still running. You did not walk then; you did not have to. The wiggle-walk moved and you just stood, or sat in one of the seats scattered along it, and let it carry you. But it had not run for a long time.

"Lew," Kristie gave a skip to catch up with her brother. Sometimes Lew walked too fast, as if he forgot that a person with shorter legs was with him. He must be thinking about something, probably something he wanted to learn more about from one of the tapes. "Lew, why doesn't the wiggle-walk run anymore? Or the elevators go up and down?"

He was frowning, not at her, but because he did not want to think about a problem.

"Because the machines that ran them all broke down," he explained. "And we don't know how to fix them." Then he began to whistle and Kristie knew he did not want to talk about it anymore.

She could guess why. Inside was run by machines. The breathers were machines, too. And the breathers, Kristie shivered—what if all the breathers broke? What would become of the Crowd then? She did not want to think about it; she would not let herself. No, she would think about her plan because, if Outside was not as Lew thought, then they could go there. And they would not have to worry about any old machines breaking down ever again!

Kristie began to sing softly to herself; her words matched Lew's whistling. He never liked music from the bing-bong tapes. Instead he learned tunes from the reading machines, just as she did. This was a nice one. She skip-hopped in time to it as she sang:

> *"London Bridge is falling down,*
> *Falling down, falling down—"*

Lew looked at her and laughed. "Like that one, do you?"
Kristie nodded but did not stop her singing:

> *"London Bridge is falling down,*
> *My fair lady!"*

Lew reached down and swung her lightly to another wiggle-walk that ran off to the side, a little below the one from their own street. Then he jumped down beside her.

"Where's London?" Kristie asked.

"Across the sea, if it's still there. When the cities were sealed, it was still one of them," Lew told her. "But after the fever we never heard from any of the other cities again. The communication center quarters were sealed. Too many people died in there and then the breather blew. We never got back to the big broadcaster again."

"Across the sea," Kristie repeated. From the tapes she knew what a sea was. A big lot of water, big enough to swallow up the whole city. Yes, she knew what the sea was, but it was hard to picture it in her mind. "I wish I could see the sea."

Lew frowned at her and shook his head. "Never again, Kristie. The cities are all sealed. Outside is poison. There are no breathers there to clean the air, so you would die."

"Why did the Olds make the air poison?"

Lew shrugged impatiently. "You know why, Kristie. They just didn't care. They let all kinds of bad things get into the air. Then, when they began to worry about what was happening, it was already too late to stop. All they could do was seal the cities. That didn't work too well either. Some breathers got bad. And there were sicknesses like the fever to kill the Olds off."

He was walking faster, as if he wanted to leave behind the bad things he could remember. Kristie, glancing at his face, did not ask any more questions. Sometimes Lew seemed to be far away, even though he was close enough for her to reach out and touch.

They came to the teaching center before Lew spoke again. As they turned in at the big door, he asked:

"What will it be today, Kristie?"

"I don't know. But I can pick for myself, Lew. You know I can run a reader just as well as you can." She wanted a chance to follow her own plan.

"All right. But don't go back home without me—" he warned.

Kristie nodded absently. She was wondering just where, among all the stacks of stored tapes, she could find some about the city. And she was very glad when Lew left her in the lower room and went off to hunt for his own material.

Kristie knew where the history tapes were. She had found some of her Outside ones there. Today she paid no attention to them. Instead she read labels here and there, searching the shelves for tapes about the city itself. And, to her joy, she finally came across a whole section with the proper labeling.

She needed early ones, she was sure. Perhaps she could find one about the sealing of the gates. Kristie made a careful selection, took the early tapes to the nearest reader, and wound the first tape into the machine.

There were three possible tapes but Kristie ran them all to make sure she had the one she wanted. The second one threw a map on the small screen. Kristie pressed the button marked "hold." She had seen maps before and knew they could be used to guide an explorer.

Now she hunched forward eagerly on the very edge of the reader seat, hunting among the map's lines for a place she already knew. There was no explain talk with the picture. Perhaps those who had taped it had not thought it necessary.

Kristie found her starting point, the very building in which she now sat. With her fingertip touching the screen, she began to trace ways branching out from the learning center. Her excitement grew as she saw that the learning center was not far, at least on the map, from a big red dot on the dome wall where it must touch ground surface.

That dot must surely mark a gate!

Kristie had a suspicion that the distance which seemed so

short on the pictured map might be much farther when one walked the stalled wiggle-walks. So she traced the map's lines in the other direction, back to the Crowd's own street. Then, with her fingers, she carefully measured the two distances and compared them as best she could.

Why it was only a teeny bit farther, just about the length of her fingernail on the map! Kristie had no idea how far a journey it could be but she guessed it was not too long.

She switched off the map after studying the three turns she must make and counting the buildings along each track where they were marked off by tiny squares. When the screen went dark, she made herself think about the map in detail. Then she switched the picture on once more to compare it with her remembered lines and squares. She had been right, recalling every bit of it!

Kristie slid off the reader seat and walked softly down the corridor of stored tapes. She could hear the steady murmur of a reader voice long before she pushed between two tall cases to peer at Lew.

He sat with his back to her, gazing steadily at the lighted screen and its pictures and listening to what seemed to be a very boring explanation about machines. Lately Lew had been more and more interested in such tapes. She wondered if he were trying to learn how to start the stalled machines. Perhaps so. There must be tapes which would tell how to do that.

However, she was more interested in the fact that he had a pile of tapes to be fed into the reader. It was plain he planned to stay for some time yet. Time enough for her to visit the gate?

Kristie was not sure. Only the longer she stayed here, just watching Lew, the more time she was wasting. So she turned and ran on tiptoe back down the long hall and out into the empty street.

This way! She turned left and hurried along, putting as much distance between herself and the learning center as she could. And as fast as she could. When she turned the second corner she slowed down a little.

It was very quiet here. Even the constant sighing of the breathers sounded faint and far away. Kristie slowed even more. Were the breathers stopped in the section through which she must pass? Well, if they were, she could turn back easily enough.

No, this was her chance to see, truly see, if there was a way Outside, and if Outside was what Lew said—all dead forever and ever.

Squaring her shoulders, Kristie marched ahead, determined to learn the truth for herself.

2

Shadows by the Gate

Here it was so lonely, so quiet—so—so—
Kristie's chin was firm. No, she was *not* afraid
of this strange part of the city. Maybe she had
never been alone before between these very tall and silent
buildings where the windows looked back at you like great
blank eyes. But really, this was just like the street where the
Crowd lived. It was!

Only—she licked her lips and clenched her hands into fists.
This was silly. Just what a Little would do—believe that now
and then something peered down at her from a window, only
to flash away when she glanced up. There was no one here!

Her feet made a padding sound on the dusty surface of
the dead wiggle-walk. Here was the second corner where she
must turn. For a moment Kristie paused and shut her eyes to
recall the map picture as fully as she could. The fact that she
could call it firmly to mind when she did this was reassuring.

Beyond was another row of tall buildings. But at ground

level were the wide shop windows. Kristie was drawn by the sight of them. Why, these still had things in the windows! Another time she might have gone looting. But she did not have the time now, not if she were to reach the gate place and be back before Lew discovered she was gone.

Her walk became a trot. She jogged along between the tempting windows, not allowing herself to examine too closely what they held. There was an echo from the thud of her feet which she did not like to hear. The sounds were strange, almost like those of the bam drum Fred liked to pound. As if something back behind those walls were drumming.

Kristie reached the second branching she must follow and stood staring ahead. There was no wiggle-walk such as threaded through the rest of the city. No, the pavement was solid, as if part of the buildings had flowed out to form it.

Also, there was no real wall to her right, just a line of narrow rods taller than she, with spaces left between them. All were locked together, top and bottom, by bars. Beyond them spread a wide-open space covered with strange, dead stuff, some of it standing tall, some matted on the ground. All was grey-brown.

Kristie approached the fenced place cautiously, wanting to see the matted stuff more closely. Perhaps these had once been growing things. She could trace trunks, branches, and long dead, dried grass.

Outside!

Then her first wild excitement quickly died. No, there was

another way beyond. This was nothing but a small piece of open space in the city itself. There was nothing green and growing as the reading tapes had shown. All was dead.

Kristie pushed her hand between the rods and reached in as far as she could to touch a tuft of grass. The blades powdered in her grasp. She jerked back and wiped her fingers on her jeans, wanting to get rid of the queer gritty stuff clinging to her skin.

Once the Olds must have tried to bring some of the Outside in. Then the growing things died. Maybe they just could not live Inside. Kristie ran her hand along the fence as she walked on. Trees and grass and bushes. She knew their names from the reading tapes and was able to distinguish each one. But all were long dead.

Seeing them dead made her feel queer. She had a hurting in her throat and her eyes smarted. What was the matter with her? Crying just like a Little because of some old dead things? She would not look at them anymore, she just would not!

Kristie focused her eyes straight ahead and moved out into the center of the solid way.

However, before she reached the end of the fence guarding the dead place, Kristie heard a sound. She swung around and looked back at the mass of dead plants and trees. There was a rustling. The noise came from the railed place and was moving towards her.

Kristie uttered a small cry of fright. She did not know exactly what she feared might be hiding in that wasteland;

she only knew that she did not want to see it! Turning, she ran over the hard surface of the solid road.

She gasped as she made a last turn to the left, rounding the end of the fence. It seemed hard to get full breaths. The blood pounded so heavily in her ears that Kristie was not sure she could hear the sighing of the breathers. She slowed to listen for the puff-puff of renewed air. Also—for the sound behind her.

There—she caught the hiss of breather air but it did not sound too even. Kristie frowned. She did not dare go on if the breathers were not good. But to go back was to fail.

Also, she thought grimly, to go back meant that she would have to repass the place of dead things. Perhaps she would even have to face what had been crawling towards her.

Kristie rubbed her hands across her sweating face. On or back? She could not just stand here forever.

The breathers were still going. They sounded slow, as if they were running down, but they were going. And right now it was easier for Kristie to head on than to turn back and see what had been moving from the dead place.

All the past experience of the Crowd cautioned her to go slowly, so that she would not use up any more air than she had to. Even if the breathers were to quit right now, she would still have enough air to get back to a safer position in the city.

She listened for any sound above the regular swish-swish which had always been a part of her life. No, nothing.

Perhaps whatever hid in that dead place would not come into the open.

By now she should be close to the gate. Kristie walked on. She listened and watched for signs that showed she was nearing her goal.

Yes!

The buildings ended. Before her was just a black greyness where the city dome curved down to meet the ground. However, breaking that curve was what must have once been an opening that was far taller than Lew and wider than the street.

But—

Kristie's vast disappointment was like being suddenly plunged into a black dark room. Across the door were wide lengths of metal welded to the frame on the top and bottom. None of the Crowd, not even Lew with his knowledge of machines, could ever hope to break through.

And there was no window in the dome so that she could see what lay on the other side of the sealed gate. Outside was gone forever.

It was only when Kristie realized this that she knew how much she had counted on there being a way out, some way of proving that the reader tapes were true. The truth must be just as Lew said. Outside was dead, killed as dead as the things she had seen only moments before. There was really no world left except Inside. The reading tapes were now all lies!

Kristie made herself go to the tall, wide gate. She put her hands on the bars that sealed it. They were real; her hopes were not.

The lump in her throat and the smarting in her eyes grew stronger. No! She was *not* going to cry. And she must never, never let anyone know how silly she had been. If Fred, Sally, Kate and that horrid Bill ever knew she believed the tapes and thought she could get Outside, they would all laugh at her.

Kristie scowled. She made a fist and pounded once against the sealing bar. Her gesture was answered by a faint hollow ring. And then came another sound which was not an echo.

She whirled about, her eyes wide with a fear which made her shiver. Her back was now to the gate. She could see clearly what was coming towards her, moving in short determined rushes. Kristie screamed.

For a long moment she was frozen in sheer terror; then she made herself move. If only she had a stunner, a bar, anything with which to face this enemy!

They were wary, approaching along shadowy places, spreading out from the dead plants. There were so many that Kristie could not count them. Grey, their teeth exposed in grins of hunger, their eyes showing red. Rats!

"No!" Kristie screamed again.

She dared not run through the lines drawing in around her. There were too many of them and they were so large! She dared not even take her eyes from them long enough to find a refuge. If she did, they might rush her.

"Lew!" Even as she screamed his name Kristie knew her voice could not reach across all the ways and buildings. Still, in the past Lew had always been there, standing between her and any danger.

She slipped along the dome's side until she came up, with a jar, against a building. Because she had nowhere else to go, Kristie now set her shoulders against it and slid along. Perhaps there was a doorway. She dared to flash a glance away from the vicious enemy and looked to her right.

Yes! There was a break in the wall. Not the door she had hoped for, but a window at the height of her shoulder. Kristie leaped for it. She had to turn her back on the rats to scramble up to whatever safety the window might offer.

There was a sharp pain in her leg. Kristie screamed again. But with a last frantic effort she pulled herself up, slamming against a slightly recessed pane of glass. It cracked and splintered. She clung, kicking at it, unmindful of any cuts. The rats squealed so wildly she could hear them as she fought against the glass barrier.

Pieces of the glass dropped from the frame. But Kristie could not enter the room beyond because there was a second smooth barrier behind the glass. She beat against it in vain. She had a narrow ledge on which to crouch and that was all.

Sobbing, Kristie edged around. The rats gathered thickly below, their heads upturned, their red eyes fixed on her. Now and then one made a determined leap. Some came near to reaching her perch.

She had blood on her cut hands and more streamed from the bite on her leg. How long could she continue to balance on the window ledge? And if she fell—

For the second time Kristie shouted "Lew!" knowing at the same time that her call would never be heard.

"Hold on!"

Kristie, unbelieving, looked away from the wave of rats fighting to reach her. Lew was coming!

He had halted on the road and was taking aim with his stunner. Below her the frantic rats began to drop and lie still. Some turned to run and were caught in the beam of Lew's weapon. They curled up limply on the stone.

When they were all still, he came swiftly forward, though he did not slip his weapon back into the loop on his belt. Kicking the unconscious rats out of his path, he held out his left hand to Kristie.

"Catch hold!" he ordered. "Jump!"

Kristie had gripped the frame of the window so tightly that her fingers were stiff and she had trouble loosening them. Somehow she scrambled down. As Lew caught her she felt very sick and queer. The buildings and even the dome wall seemed to ripple. She cried out and could not stay on her feet.

Kristie remembered very little of how they got back to their own street. Lew must have carried her most of the way while she continued to feel sick and giddy. Then, later, she lay on her bed and Fanna came to bandage her cut hands and the bite on her leg.

She awoke, finally, feeling lightheaded but no longer sick. Her leg was very sore when she moved it and her hands were wound about with strips of white bandage.

When she turned her head on the pillow she saw Lew. He was sprawled out in the big chair, his head forward on his chest and his eyes closed as if he were asleep.

"Lew?" Kristie spoke his name.

At the sound of her voice his eyes opened. He looked at her. His face was tired, as if he had been hurt, too. Kristie pulled herself higher on her pillow. Had the rats come after them? Hurt Lew? She could not see any bandages on him.

"Lew—?"

He frowned at her. Now he sat up straight and leaned a little forward.

"Why, Kristie—why did you run away?" His voice sounded as if he were really mad at her.

Kristie shivered. Lew was not usually like this; he made her feel so alone now.

"Why, Kristie?" he repeated, his voice louder and sharper.

"The gate," she said, knowing that she must answer, even if she could not make him understand. "I wanted to find the gate—Outside."

"What about the gate?"

"I wanted to see—to know—what was Outside."

Lew shook his head as if he could not understand. "But you do know, Kristie. I've told you over and over. There's nothing Outside. The world is dead. I guess I've been to blame. I should never have let you use the readers. You believed those tapes. And they aren't true—now they're just stories, Kristie, made-up stories." He thumped his knee with his fist at every word, as if by such hammering he could make her believe him. "All stories, Kristie."

"Not in the old days," she held to her small dream. "And nobody really knows even now. Nobody's been Outside for a long time."

"Nobody will ever be again," Lew got up. "And you—Kristie, you could have been—" he stopped abruptly. Then he continued, "You must stay in the street here and never go away without me or Fanna or some other Big with you. Not again."

"All right," Kristie agreed in a small voice. She knew he was right. She had gone by herself and there had been nothing to discover after all, nothing but a sealed gate and a dead place full of rats. Kristie shivered.

She must do as Lew said. Lew was always right.

3

Reddy

Kristie had bad dreams. Then, too, there was the day Meg came to see her and brought the fur pillow which was Meg's comfort in times of trouble. Only when Kristie touched it, she could see one of the rats jumping at her. She screamed and Fanna came running.

Kristie felt very ashamed of herself when she tried to explain. She was almost a Big and should not be afraid of any old pillow just because it felt soft and furry. Meg had gotten mad at her. She had marched away holding her pillow close and saying that it was not a rat, and if Kristie called it that she was crazy!

"Maybe I am crazy," Kristie hiccupped to Fanna. "Of course the pillow is not a rat. But it is furry and black, which makes me think, even see in my mind, the rats slipping in and out of shadows."

As she choked out her words, Kristie began to shake, her hands clutching tightly at the covers. Fanna gathered her close and held her until she felt warm again inside.

That evening Lew brought her Reddy. Perhaps Fanna had asked him to find something to make the dreams go away. Or maybe he knew what Kristie needed without being told.

The ever-glow lights were turned up when he came in holding a full shoulder tote as if he had been looting. Eagerly Kristie sat up in bed, hoping he had some treat for her.

However, when he shook the tote and the object it held fell on the bed, she shrank back.

Lew did not reach out to comfort her as Fanna had done. He stood still and watched Kristie stare at what he had brought. She began to shiver again and pulled herself up higher on the pillows to get away from that—that thing!

Then Lew moved. He took her hand in his. Though Kristie struggled, she did not have the strength to pull away from him. Then he drew her fingers down to touch the animal that sat there watching her with knowing black eyes.

"This is Reddy," Lew said with authority in his voice. "You remember Reddy from the story tapes."

Kristie's mouth felt dry, making it hard for her to answer. Lew continued to hold her hand firmly down on the head of the stuffed toy. It was hard for her to believe it was not alive, since Reddy looked exactly like those animals she had seen on one of her favorite story tapes.

"Reddy—" she repeated the name in a very low voice, which quavered a little. "Reddy, the fox."

Foxes once lived Outside, just as did all the other animals she so longed to see: the deer, bears, cats, dogs, and rabbits. Why, she could sit right here and name maybe fifty animals she had learned about from the tapes.

But Reddy, this Reddy, must be alive! He was so exactly like the pictures. His fur was soft under her fingers which Lew still held against Reddy's head. And he did not look like a rat in the least.

"He could kill those old rats!" Kristie said.

Lew nodded. "He sure could, or the real Reddy could. But this Reddy is yours, Kristie. And he will keep those dream rats away." Lew took away his hand, leaving hers free. Now she had no desire to snatch her fingers from the fur.

Reddy had been made to sit on his haunches, his bush of a tail curling around the side of his body. His head was cocked a little to one side, as if he watched something very interesting and was figuring out in his mind just what was to be done.

Kristie grabbed him close and with her forefinger traced his upturned ears, his button of a black nose, the sharp angle of his muzzle. He was a lovely burnished reddish brown color except for some darker spots and the white tip on the generous fluff of his tail. And, though Kristie had no way of guessing, he was life-size. She knew that he was indeed big enough to vanquish any rat which tried to face him.

"I wish—I wish he was real!" she said longingly.

Lew smiled but shook his head slowly. "Not anymore, Kristie. But you can pretend he is real."

She gathered Reddy into the crook of her arm, no longer aware of the bad memories any touch of fur brought. Reddy was the nicest thing Lew had ever given her.

"Where did you find him?" she asked. Lew was smart; he was a good looter. But he had never brought back anything as satisfying to the eye, as soft and comforting to the touch, as Reddy.

"In a store, sitting 'way up on a top shelf—" Lew gestured to show how high the shelf must have been. "He gave me a big surprise, he looked so real, just sitting there as if he were watching me."

"He was, you know," Kristie smoothed Reddy's fur. "Maybe he knew you wanted to find someone like him. He made you turn and look up to right where he was—"

Lew laughed. "Kristie, your imagination is just too big." Then the happy lights went out of his eyes as he gazed down at her. Now he was stern and serious. "You remember your promise, Kristie?"

She nodded. "I'm not to go away from the street without a Big. But the gate's no good anyway, Lew. I know that and I wouldn't try to go again. Only—" Deep down inside her the old discontent stirred again. "I wish we could know, really know what it is like Outside. I wish there were a window in the dome somewhere and we could look through it to see for ourselves."

"Kristie!" his tone was very sharp. "You promised!"

"I know. I won't go hunting any window, Lew, truly I won't. Only—don't you wish sometimes that you could see, too? The tapes—"

Lew shook his head. "No. I've seen the last tapes showing

what was Outside when the gates were finally closed. You saw those too, Kristie. Everything is dead out there, poisoned. There's nothing left but bad air we cannot breathe and dead ground."

"Yes," Kristie agreed doubtfully. But one part of her still wanted to know. Even Lew admitted those tapes were old. Could Outside have changed any? Well, she supposed there was no way of ever finding out. Now there were only picture tapes to pretend by. And she had Reddy, who was very important indeed.

Lew was called out of the room. Kristie lay back on her pillows, her face turned admiringly towards Reddy. Why had someone made Reddy look so alive? Was it because the maker missed the Outside and wanted to remember animals like foxes? Just as she, Lew, and the others watched the picture tapes?

Were there other Outside things, other animals, to be found in the city if one looked closely enough? Perhaps she could persuade Fanna, or one of the other Bigs, to go hunting with her when her leg was well.

Kristie knew that Fanna had worried about the bite. The Big girl had gone looting for medicine and now the pain was no longer a steady throb. Kristie just noticed it if she moved her leg too quickly without thinking. The glass cuts on her hands were already so well healed that she did not have to wear bandages over them anymore. But she could see the pink scars as she patted and smoothed Reddy.

Suddenly her attention was drawn away from Lew's gift as she overheard raised voices in the next room.

"First three Littles gone. Then that girl Bet who was in charge and with her two more—" The voice was a strange one. Kristie listened more closely. She even crawled to the other end of the bed to hear. Her door was ajar but not far enough to let her see who the stranger was.

"I give it to you straight," his angry voice continued, "that guy's out to get us all. And I don't think he's pill-happy either. At least, from what I've been able to pick up, he doesn't act that way. Also, any hip doesn't care about collecting Littles. They're so sunk in their private whirl-worlds they don't care about anything *real* anymore. No, I don't know where this Rhyming Man comes from or what his game is, but we've got to stop him. And we did trail him through those back alleys into your territory."

"All right," Lew answered. "I'll turn out a search party and we'll go through the alleys but good. You're welcome to bring in all you want of your Crowd to help."

"Fair enough. When can we start now?"

"As soon as I can round up our guys—"

"No girls," the other cautioned. "Seems like they can be hypoed, or whatever this guy does, just the same as the Littles."

"No girls," Lew agreed. "The trouble is right now we have three looting parties out for supplies. I don't have too many Bigs to call on. But the others can join us when they come back."

"All I want is to nail this Rhyming Man and nail him good." To Kristie the stranger's voice sounded not only angry but a little scared. "Maybe then we can make him tell where he took the Littles and our girls. So try to stun him but don't do anything fancy."

"Right. We'll get to the end of the 450th block as soon as we can muster."

There was the sound of a door closing. Then Kristie heard Fanna's voice ask:

"What do you think, Lew?"

"I don't know. According to Brad this so-called Rhyming Man comes around singing and he gets Littles to follow him. Then he and they just disappear. Brad's Crowd has lost five Littles and two girls so far. It sounds bad to me. Now Brad thinks this guy is in our territory. You make sure our own Littles stay right in the street. No going beyond."

"Of course."

Kristie heard the door close again. Lew must have left. A Rhyming Man who came around singing? Singing what? And where did he go with the Littles and Bigs who followed him?

Once more Kristie shivered as she crawled back to her pillows and huddled down into the covers with Reddy sitting by her shoulder on alert guard. She stroked him, somehow sure that she was not going to have that bad dream about rats again.

Lew did not return until very late at night, though night and day were the same thing in the city, at least out on the street where the glow-lights did not dim.

In the morning Fanna said that Kristie was well enough to get up and brought her new jeans and a shirt to wear. Her shirt was green, which was Kristie's favorite color. The material felt silky as Kristie fingered it. There was still a bandage on her leg but the jeans covered it. So she looked the same as always in Fanna's big mirror.

Reddy looked even brighter red against the green of Kristie's shirt as she cradled him in her arms. He was so real. If he were only alive like the Reddy in the reading tapes!

As Fanna came in with some soup and bread (it was fruit bread out of a loot can), Kristie said,

"Fanna—could you make Reddy come alive?"

She had dreamed while Reddy was on guard by her pillow, a wonderful, happy dream—not one to make her wake shivering with fear. She had been in a place as green as her new shirt. Reddy had been leaping back and forth ahead of her, urging her on to follow him to some exciting discovery. And she was sure that this was the Outside Lew said was dead.

Fanna tossed her heavy hair back over her shoulders. She set the tray down on the table.

"No." Fanna never talked much, except about the things which mattered most to her—helping any Little or Big who was sick or hurt. She spent almost as much time at the learning center as Lew did. But she did not hunt out tapes about machines. Rather, she was absorbed by those on helping sick people. Once or twice Kristie had seen her angry because the tapes did not teach her enough, or because she could not understand some of the words or how to use all the healing machines. (There were machines to mend broken people just as there were machines to run the city.)

"Reddy is a toy," she said to Kristie now.

"He looks so real." Kristie set the fox carefully on the table. She had the strangest feeling that she should offer him some of her food since his intense stare was aimed at her soup bowl.

"I don't know about that." Fanna shrugged. "But you are no Little to believe he is real, Kristie. You are big enough to understand the truth."

Kristie spooned up the soup. Fanna was good when you were sick or afraid, as she had been about the bad rat dream. Only when you were well again, she sometimes made you feel as if you were wasting her time.

"He looks *real*," Kristie muttered under her breath.

She could just see him stand up on his four legs, uncurl his tail, and open his mouth.

He could not talk, of course, like the Crowd. How had foxes talked to each other Outside, she wondered? What kind of noises had they made when they asked their own questions? She had never paid particular attention to animal language when she'd watched the tapes; she had always been more interested in how the Outside creatures lived.

Kristie wished that there had been a window at the gate so she could have seen for sure that there was nothing left Outside.

"The Olds made a lot of things which looked real but weren't," Fanna said. It sounded a little as if she did not like the idea of real-unreal things.

Then she spoke directly to Kristie. "I have to go see Ella now.

You can go down to the street if you want to, Kristie. But remember what you promised Lew."

"I know. And I won't—leave the street, I mean." Kristie watched Reddy rather than Fanna, who was putting some small bottles into a bag. Kristie knew Ella was often ill. That was one reason Fanna read the tapes about healing. She hoped to find answers in them to help Ella. Fanna and Ella had been Littles together, and Fanna worried a lot about her.

Kristie finished her soup and ate all the bread, which was a real treat. The Crowd did not find much bread anymore. She washed her bowl and spoon in the sink under a slow trickle of water. The water seemed to run more slowly every time she ran it. Lew worried about the water a lot.

As she set the bowl on a shelf, Kristie wondered what would happen if the water stopped running altogether. What would they drink then, and how could they wash? Lew said some parts of the city were already dead. Maybe the Crowd would have to move to another part of the city if the water failed.

Kristie gathered up Reddy and went down to the street. Bill and Meg were there and some of the real Littles. Kathie had the twins sitting by her and was telling them a story. There were only three *real* Littles anymore. Lew said they had been born just at the end of the plague time. After they grew up, there would be no more Littles.

The Bigs would grow to be Olds and she and the other Littles would grow to be Bigs. Kristie sat down on the edge of the dead wiggle-walk and for the first time wondered what would happen to them all in the future. Another plague? Or would the whole city just stop?

She felt cold when her mind made those pictures. If parts of Inside were dead now, how long would it take for everything to stop? No water, no food, no breathers. Kristie began to feel just as she had when she had seen the rats moving in on her—as if she wanted to run away screaming, and yet could not move. This was a very bad feeling; it made her sick and giddy.

4

London Bridge Is Falling Down

i!"
Bill was running down the wiggle-walk, bouncing a ball ahead of him. Now he paused by Kristie.

She looked up warily. Bill teased a lot. Sometimes he was really mean. She was not sure she even liked Bill.

"Hi," she answered.

"What you got there?" He leaned over her, eyeing Reddy with interest.

Kristie laced her fingers protectively around Reddy.

"A fox." She made her answer as brief as she could. She wished he would go away.

Bill grinned. "A fox?" He tossed his ball from one dirty hand to the other. "Where'd you get it?"

"Lew brought it."

"Let's see it—" He stuffed his ball in his pocket, reached out—

Kristie dodged. "No, Reddy's mine." Suddenly she was afraid again.

Bill was wearing his going-to-be-mean look.

"I just want to see it." He advanced on her. "I won't hurt your old fox. Give us a look now—"

"No!" Kristie tried to stand up. But she was still shaky from being sick and her leg hurt as she jerked away, trying to evade Bill's grabbing hands.

Then she caught her toe on the edge of the wiggle-walk and sprawled forward. Reddy fell out of her grasp. She could not squirm around in time to prevent Bill's scooping up the fox.

To Kristie's horror, Bill tossed Reddy up in the air and yelled: "Flying fox! See the flying fox!"

Kristie scrambled up and rushed at him. But he had already caught Reddy once more and was swinging the fox behind his back. Now he twisted and turned as he danced backward just beyond Kristie's reach.

"Give it to me!" She was so mad she was nearly crying. "Bill, you give me Reddy!"

"Yeah, come and get him!" Bill yelled back. "If you want this old fox, you've got to get him."

He turned. Holding Reddy tightly against his chest, he began to run down the wiggle-walk. Kristie limped after him. She doubted she could catch up with Bill. And even if she did, he was bigger and stronger than she. But she must try as hard as she could to get Reddy back.

Bill reached the end of the block. He looked back at her, still grinning in that hateful way. Once more he tossed Reddy up in the air and called:

"Flying fox!"

Tears now slipped down Kristie's cheeks. She rubbed angrily at her eyes. Bill liked to see her cry. Listen to him now!

Bill was jumping up and down, his hand around Reddy's neck, swinging the fox back and forth as if the animal were a ball bat.

"Yah, Yah! Kristie's a crybaby! Lookit the crybaby!"

With a last "crybaby," he rounded the house at the block's end. Forgetting her promise to Lew and Fanna, Kristie limped after Bill as fast as she could. As she passed the corner, she saw Bill waiting for her halfway down the street, once more tossing Reddy up in the air.

This time he caught Reddy by the tail and swung the fox around and around. Kristie cried out.

She knew Reddy was not really alive but somehow he

seemed so to her. To see Bill swinging him by his bushy tail was as horrible as if Reddy could feel the pain.

"No, don't!" she screamed.

Bill only laughed.

"Crybaby!" he jeered. "You think you're so smarty-smart 'cause your brother's the Big Man for the Crowd. Well, I've got no big brother, but I'm a lot smarter 'n faster 'n everything than any old girl. Isn't that so, Kristie? Isn't it? Say it—say it! That I'm smarter than you! If you don't, you won't see this old stuffed thing again!"

He swung Reddy around harder and harder. Then, to Kristie's terror and despair, Reddy's body arched far up into the air, though his bush of a tail still remained in Bill's tight hold. Up and out flew Reddy, back into the open mouth of one of the small passages between two buildings, where there were dark places in spite of the overhead lights.

"Stupid old thing." After a moment of silence Bill dropped the tail and gave the piece of fur a kick. "Just a silly thing for a Little to play with."

But he was no longer grinning. Instead he looked uneasy, eyeing Kristie sideways.

"Stupid thing!" he repeated loudly, and started down the street towards her. But he kept to the other side, still watching the girl as if he expected her to call one of the Bigs to deal with him.

Bill—Bill had *killed* Reddy! Kristie paid no attention to the boy as he edged past, well away from her. She felt queer inside, as if something so terrible had happened that she could not think about it. She did not even see Bill leave. Her eyes were fixed on the tail lying on the wiggle-walk.

Kristie limped on until she could pick it up. Now she was shocked past crying. She just felt all cold inside. The furry tail was in her hands. But Reddy—Reddy was gone!

For a long minute Kristie stood there, trying not to believe that this awful thing had happened. Only she could not shut out the truth. Reddy—!

Kristie turned to face the narrow, shadow-filled passageway into which the fox had disappeared. Maybe she could find him. She had to find him!

Holding the tail tightly in her sweating hand, Kristie plunged into the dark way. She stumbled over a clutter of broken-open boxes. Looters must have used this way for a dump. How could she ever find Reddy in this mass of debris?

Kristie forced herself to go slowly and look carefully. Her leg ached as she climbed over and around boxes and ripped-open cartons, pushing and pulling at some so she could see better into the cracks between them.

How could Reddy have flown so far? Kristie was more than halfway down the alley now. Somehow she must have missed him.

"Reddy?" She called in a thin voice as if he could really hear her and answer. Now she was crying again, wearily, as she looked around. There were so many places where he might be and she could not see him.

Her only hope was to search clear to the end of the way and then come back again.

She kicked at paper which lay in dirty wads and rounded a couple of crates with mashed-in ends. She had to stop and rest her leg. It hurt so much now. She leaned against a pile of boxes, with tears so heavy in her eyes that she could no longer see very well.

It was when she started to search again that she caught a glimpse of ruddy fur. With a cry of relief Kristie pulled at a carton. Reddy!

He had landed on his back and was looking up at her with his shining black eyes. Kristie hugged him close.

"Reddy!"

Perhaps Fanna could put on his tail. Reddy might not be alive like Kristie or Ella, but he was a person to Kristie and he needed Fanna to help him.

She turned him around to inspect where the tail had come loose. There was a hole, and on the tail was a point which must fit into the hole. Kristie gently pushed Reddy's tail into its rightful place. It was still loose. She would have to be very careful until Fanna could fasten it, maybe with some glue. But Reddy was whole again. And as Kristie examined him, she could discover no further harm.

"Reddy!" She hugged him tightly. Now that she had time to think she was really mad at Bill. She did not usually tattletale to a Big, but Kristie decided that she must let Lew know about Bill.

She held Reddy tenderly against her as she rose from the crate where she had been sitting. She felt so relieved and happy that she began to sing one of the songs from the tapes. It was the same one Lew had whistled on the day she had hunted for the Gate:

> "London Bridge is falling down,
> Falling down, falling down."

Suddenly Kristie was startled into silence. Someone else was singing, and it was not a Little. The voice was strong and deep:

> "Who will build it up again,
> Up again, up again?"

The other voice sang loud and clear.

Kristie wet her lips with her tongue tip.

"Lew?" she called uncertainly. But Lew seldom sang; he preferred to whistle. Could it be one of the other Bigs? No, she had never heard any of them sing that kind of a song.

> "We shall build it up again,
> Up again, up again!
> We shall build it up again,
> My fair lady!"

Then she heard more voices—Littles' voices!

With Reddy pressed tightly to her for safety, Kristie headed on down the way towards the voices instead of back towards the block where the Crowd lived.

> *"Wood and clay will wash away,*
> *Wash away, wash away—"*

It was the deep voice again. The Littles echoed in their shriller tones:

> *"Wood and clay will wash away,*
> *My fair lady!"*

The singing was now quite close. Kristie halted at the end of the alley and looked out onto a more brightly lighted and wider wiggle-walk. She gasped at what she saw.

There was a Big—no, he was an *Old!* But there were no Olds left; everyone knew that. Then how could she be seeing one?

He was not walking or running but jigging along, two steps forward and one back, hopping from foot to foot. His tall body was never still. Sometimes he faced ahead. Sometimes he turned around in a jump to look back the way he had come, at those who followed him.

He had followers—four Littles! Two were perhaps as old as Kristie herself, the other two younger. And as they sang, they were hopping and jiggling along, too, just like the Old.

As he jumped, spun, and danced, his body glittered all over. He was not wearing the same kind of clothes as the Crowd. His clothes fitted tightly to his body and were patched with different colors. The patches shone as if sewn with sparkles. Little flickers of light ran from one patch to the next with every movement of the Old's body.

As he waved his arms and flipped his hands back and forth, the sparks of color seemed to spring out into the air around him. His head bobbed and nodded. It was covered with hair as white as the cotton thread Fanna used to sew with. One lock flopped down until it almost hid his twinkling eyes. And his brown skin was darker than any Kristie had ever seen before.

"'Iron and steel will rust away,'" he continued the song, waving one arm urgently as if telling them to sing louder.

"'Rust away, rust away!'" the Littles shouted in return.

Then he glanced around and his eyes met Kristie's.

He—she did not know what happened at the moment when he looked at her so directly. There was something very important which she must do, which they all must do.

Lew—Fanna—for a short second she remembered her promise. Then the memory was swept away.

The sparkling Old was beckoning to her. He was not singing now, but smiling gently. Why, there was nothing at all to be afraid of. This was right: to follow the Rhyming Man was what she wanted to do most in all the world.

She moved out of the shadowed alley. The Rhyming Man was never still, even as he paused to wave her on to join the Littles. Instead he hopped and skipped, smiled and nodded.

> "In and out do we go,
> Bow and scrape,
> And point the toe!"

He sang, pointing to her and the rest of the Littles and making them a deep bow. He ended by following his own orders and pointing outward with his toe on the walk.

> *"Take hands, all,*
> *And let us go!*
> *Time is short,*
> *That we know."*

Kristie shifted Reddy into the crook of her right arm and found her left hand caught by the nearest Little. Now they were all linked together.

The Rhyming Man nodded so vigorously as he viewed them that sparkles of color appeared to fly outwards from every part of him.

"*'London Bridge is falling down,'*" he began once more.

Kristie began to dance in time to the tune, her hurting leg quite forgotten as she joined in singing:

"*'Falling down, falling down—'*"

Now she neither knew nor cared where they might be going—just following the Rhyming Man was enough.

5

In and Out, Roundabout

> *"Trip and go, heave and ho!*
> *Up and down, to and fro;*
> *From the town to the grove,*
> *Two by two let us rove,*
> *A-maying, a-playing;*
> *Love hath no gainsaying!*
> *So—merrily, merrily, trip and go!"*

The Rhyming Man jigged along. And though Kristie had never heard the song before, she was singing the words as if she had known them all her life. The girl she held hands with was singing, too, as were all the Littles. The sound of their voices filled the street and echoed back from the empty buildings.

Kristie was only dimly aware that this was a part of the city she had never seen before. Many of the lights were out so that shadows crept out toward them over the edge of the wiggle-walk on which they danced. However, the glimmer of the Rhyming Man's clothing grew brighter and brighter. He was like a moving light leading them on.

"'*Here we go round the jingo-ring,*'" he sang as he pranced to the left into a wide doorway of one of the buildings.

> "*The jingo-ring, the jingo-ring.*
> *Here we go round the jingo-ring,*
> *With a merry-ma, merry-ma-tanzie!*"

The inside of the building was light again. This radiance spread, not from the walls or the ceiling far over their heads, but from under their feet. When they danced after their singing leader into a great room, Kristie saw that the floor was made up of big blocks of different colors. As the Rhyming Man jigged and hopped from one to the next, the blocks blazed under his feet.

Somehow Kristie and the rest knew, without his ever telling them, that they must follow him carefully, stepping in turn just where he had gone. Now he dropped back to catch hands with the two smallest Littles, turning a wide smile from one to the other.

> "*See-saw, sacaradown,*
> *Now which is the way to London*
>   *Town?*
> *Put one foot up, the other down.*
> *This is the way to London Town!*"

There was a red square beneath Kristie, then a yellow. Now a green, then a blue. The Rhyming Man hopped two squares to the left and landed on another red one, carrying both Littles with him as easily as if they had springs on their feet. Yellow again, then another hop to the right, not this time to blue but to a block which glowed green, then over farther to a red.

Kristie did not try to think about what they were doing. She simply followed the feeling that this was right. Her feet obeyed the movements of the Rhyming Man with no commands from her to do this or that.

> "Intery, mintery, cutery corn;
> Appleseed and apple thorn;
> Wine, brier, lumber-lock,
> Five fat geese in one flock.
> Sit you now and let us sing,
> Out about and in again!"

He had dropped the Littles' hands and they squatted down on the floor, each in the middle of a red block. Kristie was planted on a yellow. The others, flanking her, were on green.

For the first time the Rhyming Man stood still. Now the smile left his face as he turned to look at them one after another, staring straight into the eyes of each of his small followers. When his gaze met Kristie's, she was not afraid but rather excited, the way a person gets when something good is about to happen.

He began to sing again, but this time none of the children recognized the words or believed they must sing, too.

> *"For every evil under the sun,*
> *There is a remedy, or there is none.*
> *If there be one, seek till you find it,*
> *If there be none, never mind it."*

Kristie did not know just what he meant. However, she sensed that this was important. They must do something now—she waited for the Rhyming Man to tell them what it was.

> *"Seeing's believing—no, no, no!*
> *Believing's seeing, you can go!"*

Kristie was puzzled. She was sure that what he said was very important indeed. Yet she could not understand.

Again he was quiet and looked at each of them for a long, searching moment. Then once more he smiled. Kristie let go of her breath in a sigh of relief. It was all right; her not understanding did not really matter in the least. She should just follow the Rhyming Man and all would be well.

He snapped his fingers. The Littles understood his signal and scrambled once more to their feet. He skipped from one red block to the next, always facing them.

"'*Now we dance, looby, looby, looby,*'" his voice seemed to fill the whole of the room, big as it was.

> *"Now we dance, looby, looby, looby,*
>   *light.*
> *Look to your left hand,*
> *Now to your right!"*

Like the others, Kristie obeyed, moving first to the nearest block to the left and then right to the one she had stood on before. Twice the Rhyming Man sang directions, and twice they did just as he told them.

Then he was still, raising his hand with a long finger ready to point.

> *"Eeery, Orrey, Ickery, Ann,*
> *Fillison, Follison, Nicholas John,*
> *Queevy, Quavey, English Navy,*
> *Out goes you—and you—and*
>   *you—"*

His finger moved very quickly, pointing at first to the two Littles right before him, then at those on a line with Kristie. She did not even have time to gasp as she saw one child after another disappear. Then—

Kristie had no words to describe what happened when that long finger centered on her. There was no light, just a big, thick black in which she was lost. She tried to scream, and then—

She was rolling across something as green as the blocks of the pavement, but much softer. It did not shine either.

As Kristie came to a halt, she lay on her back looking up.

There was no grey dome over her. Kristie gulped. Was that—*sky?* Could she be—*Outside?*

She shut her eyes. No! This was so—so open! If this was really Outside, she did not want to be here after all. Lew! She wanted Lew! She wanted Fanna. She wanted most of all to open her eyes and again see the buildings, the wiggle-walk, all that was right and real. Not this—this emptiness!

Clutching Reddy tightly to her, Kristie tried to believe that this was all a bad dream, like her dreams about the rats. It must be a dream—it must be!

> "For every evil under the sun,
> There is a remedy, or there is none.
> If there be one, seek till you find it.
> If there be none, never mind it."

The Rhyming Man's voice. Now the words sounded fainter, as if he were farther away. No hollow echo followed as it had in the big hall.

Kristie knew she could not sit here forever holding her eyes shut. So she made herself think about the words of the song, even though she did not understand them.

Summoning up all her courage, Kristie opened her eyes. There was the Rhyming Man, looking straight at her again. Only she did not feel as confident as she had when he had gazed at her that way before. Outside, his bright clothing did not glitter and his face looked as if he were very tired— somehow a little like Lew looked when he was worried about the breathers stopping or the machines going wrong.

Behind him, all around him, the world was green! Not the bright green of the squares over which they had danced, but a green Kristie had never seen before.

She swallowed again. It was true. This was Outside—as it had been on the reading tapes. That was a tree right behind the Rhyming Man, this was grass under her—

All this openness—no walls, no dome. Kristie crouched lower, hugging the ground, wanting the walls, the dome. They were safe—this was—

She heard a babble of voices and turned her head very cautiously. They were all there, all the others who had followed the Rhyming Man. But now they were strangers. Kristie hugged Reddy tighter. She was fighting tears and she wanted to scream as loudly as she had when the rats caught her.

The Rhyming Man still looked down into her eyes. Kristie tried to avoid his gaze. No! She would not—

He was pointing once more. Not at her this time but up into the open sky.

> "Star light, star bright,
> First star I've seen tonight.
> I wish I may, I wish I might,
> Have the wish I wish tonight."

Against her will, but because she somehow had to look where his finger pointed, Kristie once more raised her head to blink at the sky. It was darker now. There was a twinkle of light far, far above.

A star! A real star!

Her wonder fought her fear. She knew what a star was though no one in the city had ever seen one, not even the long-gone Olds. It had been years, and years, and years—so many even Lew could not hope to count them—since the dome had gone up to close out the sky and the rest of the world. But here was a star!

Somehow, staring at that distant wink of light, which was not as bright as the glitter of the Rhyming Man's clothing yet sharp in another way, Kristie became less and less afraid.

Reddy's head was soft and furry under her chin as she wavered up to her knees and then got to her feet.

"This is Outside." She said the words almost as if she were asking the Rhyming Man a question.

> "Outside, inside,
> Front to back.
> Starlight, Sunlight—
> There is no lack."

Slowly Kristie allowed her eyes to slip away from the star and move across that very frightening sweep of sky which was not a big, safe cover like the dome but only a big, big emptiness.

No! There was another star! And this one she had found for herself. Maybe it was hers to wish on. Or did only that first star count?

"You said—wish." She looked now to the Rhyming Man.

He smiled again and nodded eagerly. But he stood quietly. Out here on the green grass, he no longer danced.

"I wish Lew were here!" Kristie had been encouraged by the Rhyming Man's smile. "He said—he said there was no Outside anymore. I want Lew!"

She did want him fiercely. Not just to prove that the Outside was alive and (as she was beginning to guess) a very wonderful place. No, she wanted Lew because he was the closest person she had ever known. He was her own Big.

The Rhyming Man no longer smiled. His eyes, Kristie thought with a small fear beginning to grow in her, were sad.

"Lew can come? He will come!" Her question turned to a demand.

Slowly the Rhyming Man shook his head.

> "Little—Big—
> Little go, Big no.
> Always must it
> Answer so."

"Why?" demanded Kristie. Her fear was heating into anger. "Why can't a Big come here?"

"Some of us do—"

Kristie turned quickly at the sound of another voice. She had half forgotten those who had come Outside with her. Now she saw there were others with them, soothing the very small Littles who were sniffling and holding hands with the others. And right next to her stood a Big girl like Fanna.

The stranger smiled and held out her hand. "Some do, you see," she repeated. "I did."

"Who are you?" Kristie demanded bluntly.

"Lisa. And that," she pointed to another Big who had picked up one of the Littles, "is Truda. Beyond there is Sally. We are from London Town. Come—"

Kristie eyed her warily. She glanced back to where the Rhyming Man had been. There was no longer anyone there.

"Where—" her surprise now sent her toward Lisa. "Where did he go?"

"Back Inside," Lisa answered.

Her fingers curled about Kristie's in warm welcome.

"Come on, let's go to London Town."

"But Lew said that's far off across the sea. How do we get there from here?" asked Kristie.

She did not pull back, however, as the Big girl drew her around some bushes and down a slope. The light in the sky was a lot dimmer, making it harder for them to see where they were going. There seemed to be no glow-lights Outside.

"Not this London. Not where we are to build the bridge," Lisa answered.

"Lew!" Kristie halted and tried to jerk away from the gentle hold. But Lisa tightened her grip.

"If he can come—in time he will," Lisa told her.

"I wish I knew what you meant," Kristie said sadly.

"But you shall, you shall," Lisa promised as they went on. The tall-standing live grass brushed softly against their legs and the stars came winking into life over their heads.

6

Believing Is Seeing

If she had been alone, Kristie might have grown uneasy and even frightened as the night darkened. She could hear queer noises. The loudest was made by the brook as it gurgled along just a little way off. She lay beside Lisa on the heap of grass which was her bed.

There were other sounds, too. Some buzzed and some called. Each time Kristie would stiffen to listen. Lisa seemed to sense her vague fears, though Kristie said nothing. Then the older girl would explain that such and such a noise was a harmless flying thing or a small animal they did not have to fear.

Kristie kept peering into the dark which she had never seen before. Though the stars hung overhead, they were too far away to give much light. However, something else was beginning to shine—a great orange-yellow ball was rising in the sky. The moon! It must be the moon!

Once people like her, and Lew, and the Crowd had flown up to the moon. Kristie remembered a tape Lew had run in which

Olds, wearing queer thick clothing, walked with slow strides across the broken surface of the moon. The tape voice had spoken of a later moon station where people lived for a while.

But men had not stayed there long. Shortly after, the world had become so bad all the Olds went into their cities and sealed them up tight. Only—if the world had been so bad, how could Outside now be green and good again? Kristie drew a deep breath. The air Outside was different and full of strange smells, but not the bad ones you sometimes sniffed Inside. What had happened to the Outside? Why had the Olds said it was poisoned, bare, brown and dead?

"When the Olds left it," Lisa's voice came as a soft whisper through the dark, "the world began to clean itself—"

Kristie's head jerked around so that she was no longer looking at the big ball of the moon but facing Lisa through the dark. The girl's face was only a thin sliver of white which Kristie could not truly see.

"You—I did not ask about that—not out loud." Kristie shivered. She was sure she had not said a word. She had only thought. Yet Lisa answered what she was thinking about! How could that happen?

"'Believing's seeing'—" Lisa whispered. "Do you understand what that means, Kristie?"

"I—I guess not." She told the truth. The Rhyming Man had said the same thing when she asked about Lew—but she could not understand.

Lew—where was he now? What was he doing? Hunting for her? She wanted Lew!

"If he can come, he will." Again Lisa read Kristie's thoughts.

Holding Reddy tightly, as if he were the only real thing she had left, Kristie sat up on the grass bed. Again the feeling of being lost in a big open place where there were no safe walls closed in on her.

Lisa moved too. But when she tried to put her arm around Kristie, the younger girl shrank away.

"I want to go home—" she muttered. "Tell the Rhyming Man—I want to go back!"

"Listen, Kristie, there is no going back," Lisa told her.

Panic flooded through Kristie. Then, before she could move away, Lisa held her in a tight hold. And—Kristie uttered a small cry, but she did not battle the arms around her.

She, Lisa, was talking to Kristie without words—in a queer way in her *mind*! There was nothing to be afraid of, Lisa was telling her. Kristie gulped. What was happening to her? Please, she cried out silently, oh, please tell me what is happening?

"We are not sure ourselves yet," Lisa whispered. She was no longer inside Kristie's head, but spoke as people always did. Somehow Kristie was no longer so scared.

"This has something to do with the way we came here," Lisa continued. "The real Littles accept it without trouble. It's only when you are older that you wonder. We do not know why this happens to us. Neither does the Rhyming Man, or else he won't explain. But when we come out of the city we begin to learn that we can understand what others are thinking—if we wish to.

"'*Believing's seeing*'—" Lisa whispered, "Rhyming Man

says. It means, Kristie, that we must not think that anything is true only because we see it in one way. We must be able to guess that things can happen which are very strange and different from everything we have known before.

"Those who follow the Rhyming Man seem able to do this. He cannot bring anyone out from the city who does not have this sort of mind. Some Bigs will never believe in what they cannot see. Those Bigs may never leave Inside. Most Littles are not yet so sure of what they are supposed to believe to say this or that may not be so. Do you understand?"

Kristie had listened closely. Yes, she could see a meaning in the words of the Rhyming Man now. It was like some of the Bigs who did not care to use the reading tapes. They argued that the reading tapes were all just made-up stories. Then there were others, such as Lew and Fanna, who hunted for knowledge. Since Kristie had so wanted to know what was Outside, her dreams could all come true.

"Like the reading tapes," she said, "are not all made-up things after all. Some of them are real if you hunt for the right ones."

"Yes. Most of us who came Outside have listened to the tapes and imagined what other ways of life would be like. So the Rhyming Man was able to make us listen and follow him. That is why we are here."

"Why does the Rhyming Man want to bring us Outside?"

"Because it is time to build again. Remember London Bridge?" Lisa repeated some of the old song:

"Build it up with stone, my dears,
Then it shall last a thousand years!"

"But you aren't really building a bridge, are you?" Kristie asked.

"Not one you can see, no," Lisa admitted. "But in a way we are the stones ourselves. And we are careful about what we build now. We want it to last at least a thousand years."

"You mean a new way of living with—Outside?"

"Yes. But we must not make the same mistakes the Olds did. We dare not poison the world a second time."

"So how do we learn not to make those mistakes?" Kristie asked.

"By thinking together—one mind to the next—in this new way. At least that is what we believe now."

The light from the big yellow moon touched Lisa's face to show her smiling.

"Lew?" Kristie could not return that smile. "And Fanna? I want them to help build London Bridge. How can I make them come?"

Lisa's smile faded. "I don't know, Kristie. If they cannot accept *'Believing's seeing'*—then they never will."

"They must!" Kristie cried fiercely. "They must!"

She allowed Lisa to settle her back on the grass bed, Reddy tight in her arms. Lew had brought the fox to her. Maybe he was not alive, but she loved him.

Kristie closed her eyes to shut out the moonlight. She would make Lisa believe she had gone to sleep. Just as she had once planned to find the gate to Outside, so now she wanted to seek a way back Inside. Not to stay, but to let Lew and Fanna and all the rest know about London Bridge.

Lisa said no one could go back Inside. But Kristie would test that for herself. Lew! As she once had shouted his name in terror when the rats came out of the dead place to hunt her, now she tried to call him in her thoughts. Could thoughts reach Inside even if people could not go back?

Though she tried to make a picture of Lew in her mind as she had once pictured the map, it was very hard. She was tired and the picture kept getting blurry. She was—Kristie was asleep.

Inside the city Lew crouched on a balcony staring down into the great hall below. The blocks of the pavement were no longer as bright as they had been when Kristie and the others had hopped and marched back and forth with the Rhyming Man.

Kristie! Lew's hand tightened about the grip of his stunner. He had returned from the search only to discover that Kristie had gone. Then the distant sound of singing echoing through the streets had guided him here. But at the door to the hall, which had looked wide open, he had run hard into an invisible wall of force that had kept him from plunging on to snatch Kristie away from the others. The Littles had all been watching the dancing, glittering Old as if he were the only real thing in the whole wide world.

It had taken Lew far too long to find this upper way from which he could look down into the hall. But as he had crept to the edge of the balcony he had seen Kristie disappear. She disappeared right before his eyes as if she had never been there at all!

They were all gone now and the blocks were dull. Gone? Where and how?

Lew tried to think clearly. There were many strange machines in the city. A lot of them did not work anymore. The Bigs who were interested did not even know what some of these machines had done.

Lew could only guess that the whole floor was one such machine. Only—what was its purpose? And where was Kristie?

Those nonsense songs and dancing from square to square—what had they to do with any machine? Lew leaned back against the wall. There were scraps of things he remembered from the readers. Now he tried to sort them out in his mind, to think calmly and coolly. What he really wanted to do was run down and beat on the squares to see if they could be trapdoors. Was Kristie now stuck in some underground passage?

That Rhyming Man—who—what—? Lew shook his head. He must forget his raging wish to use his stunner on that Old! Kristie was the only important one. He must find her.

Machines. He had read about some in the city which

would run if one spoke to them in just the right tone of voice or used the proper combination of words. Had the Rhyming Man worked some such machine here with his silly songs?

And the way the Littles under his command had changed squares. Did those changes from one color to another also start a machine working? What kind of a machine? Where had it taken Kristie and the rest?

At the end of the balcony was another stairway into the hall. Lew ran towards it, half expecting once more to meet the solid but invisible wall of force. But there was nothing to prevent his going into the hall.

He walked across the blocks, heading for those where he had last seen the Littles. Under his steps the colors also glowed bright and strong. He stooped and ran his hands over the surface of a red one. Light to be seen, but no heat to be felt.

Right about here was the place. Lew halted. Now—he must remember both the pattern in which the Littles had moved across the floor and the songs which matched their dancing. Could he do it? The boy closed his eyes and tried to re-create the scene, not as something real with Kristie a part of it, but rather as a picture on a reader screen.

When he looked about him again—

Lew swung the stunner up, ready to fire—the Rhyming Man was back. The Old pranced around, not singing this time but watching Lew with a measuring stare.

"Where's Kristie?" Lew demanded loudly, leveling the stunner. His voice echoed back at him—"Kristie?"—in a question which the Rhyming Man did not open his mouth to answer. Instead the jiggling figure chanted:

> *"Little—Big—*
> *Little go, Big no,*
> *Always must it*
> *Answer so."*

"Talk sense," Lew ordered. In spite of the way this crazy Old jumped around, Lew was sure he could beam him. But first he must make him tell how to find Kristie.

"*'Little go, Big no!'*" the Rhyming Man repeated. Now he shook his head from side to side in an exaggerated sweep, as if the gesture would impress Lew with the fact nothing could be done.

Lew reined in his temper. He could beam this Old and knock him out. Only it would be a waste of time. There was another way. He was as tall as the Old. And there was not another boy in the Crowd who could pin Lew down. This Old was really old. Lew saw how thin he was and looked at his white hair. Lew could take him easily.

With a forward rush Lew jumped at the Old.

He struck, not against the other's slight body, but against the floor with a force which made him grunt. His rush towards the Old had made him bump into the same kind of force wall as the one that had prevented his saving Kristie. The stunner flew from his hand, skidded across the smooth block, and landed at the Old one's feet.

Lew tensed, waiting for a return attack. All the Old had to

do was reach down and pick up the stunner. Then he could give Lew a blast which would keep him quiet while the Old went off to collect more Littles.

However, the Rhyming Man made no effort to pick up the weapon. He did not even look at it. Instead he stared at Lew.

At first, Lew thought the Old seemed to be hunting for something in the boy's expression. Then the Rhyming Man gave a small shrug. His face changed and looked tired and old, as if he had just faced some disappointment.

Lew licked his lips. He had to know about Kristie. He had to!

"Kristie—where's Kristie?" he repeated the question he had asked earlier, but this time in despair. The Old would never tell him and this was what he feared most.

"*For every evil under the sun,*'" the Old was mouthing one of those fool rhymes again but Lew, always hoping, listened closely.

> "*There is a remedy, or there is none.*
> *If there be one, seek till you find it.*
> *If there be none, never mind it.*"

'*Seek till you find it*'? That was what he was trying to do. And never, never would Lew admit there was none and not mind it!

Suddenly the Rhyming Man's expression changed again. He gave a quick, sharp nod as if Lew had said something to which he agreed. And he gave one of his quick sidewise jumps as he proclaimed loudly:

"Seeing's believing—no, no, no!
Believing's seeing, you can go!"

He twirled around and was gone, right before Lew's wide open eyes!

7

It Will Last a Thousand Years

"Seeing's believing—no, no, no!
Believing's seeing, you can go!"

Lew repeated the words, trying to make some sense of them. He could guess that they had importance. Now, as he sat on the floor where his attack on the Old had thrown him, he looked around in search of something —anything—which could be a clue.

" '*Seeing's believing*'—" he said slowly for the second time. He believed in what he saw. He saw this hall and blocks which flared into color when he stepped on them. This was real, solid. He could pound his fist down on the block before him and feel its unyielding surface against his hand.

" 'No, *no*, *no*'—" Why "no"? Did the Rhyming Man mean not to believe in what I saw?

Lew was suddenly certain that this was the truth. Then, if he were not to believe in what he saw, he was to believe in what he did not see! Of course, this would be believing as seeing!

Was this what had happened to Kristie and the rest? They had believed in the Rhyming Man and in what might not be real. So they went. Went—where? Somewhere else in the city, surely. But *where*?

What must you believe *in*?

Lew looked to where the stunner lay just as it had fallen at the Rhyming Man's feet. Machines—the stunner was a tool, a machine. The whole city was a machine to keep life going on in a burnt-out world. This hall was a machine and machines followed set patterns, planning—if he could discover the secret of the pattern, then he could make it work for him and reach Kristie.

The pattern must have something to do with the way the Littles had moved under the direction of the Rhyming Man. Perhaps the songs with their strings of nonsense words were also a part of it. Maybe the sounds of the words helped to activate the machine. If Lew could only remember!

"*Believing's seeing*"—he must *believe* that this would work. This was the most important thing of all.

He got to his feet but did not move to pick up the stunner.

Instead he turned slowly and completely around so that he could see all the blocks of the pavement. Then he drew a deep breath—

Here goes!

Red square, yellow, blue—

No! Lew halted on a blue which had not blazed to light when he stepped on it. Something was wrong. Nor could he remember the first song at all. Its words had been muffled by the walls as he was trying to find a way in. If only the Rhyming Man—

Lew swung back again to eye the portion of the floor where the Old had danced. Just the stunner lay there to mark the spot.

"Hi—" Lew's voice rang hollowly. "Hi, there!" He did not even know what name to call the Old. "Rhyming Man!" he shouted at last. Only the echo answered him.

Lew stood straight, head high, his fists on his hips, facing the emptiness as if it were an enemy. He was not licked, not with Kristie missing! Then, as if something deep inside him moved, he called aloud again, not for the strange Old, but for his sister:

"Kristie!"

Outside, the moon was now high and bright. Kristie shifted on the pile of grass. She opened her eyes. A dream—a dream about Lew. Lew!

Softly she crawled away from the nest beside Lisa. Lew wanted her. She knew this as well as if she could hear him call. On her hands and knees she crept from the place where the others slept.

Once up the slope she got to her feet and began to scramble higher as fast as she could. If she could just discover the place where she had come Outside, then she could find Lew. She must find Lew!

At the top of the rise Kristie looked carefully around. There, she was sure she remembered that tree. She had seen it behind the Rhyming Man when she asked him about Lew. Only there was no gate Outside—just open country. She turned to glance back. Far in the opposite direction was a big, black blot which swallowed the land. Even where the moon shone down on it the light was less clear. The city!

Kristie studied the blot. So that was what the city looked like—dirty and dark. She shivered. And Lew was caught in there, with Fanna and all the others. No! Lew must come out!

Lew! She did not scream his name aloud as she had when the rats had cornered her by the sealed gate. Instead she made a picture of Lew in her mind and called to it with her thoughts in a way she had never tried before.

She *saw* Lew.

He was standing in the hall where the colored blocks made the floor. Lew had found the Rhyming Man's place and was going to come Outside!

Happiness flooded through Kristie. Then she realized that Lew was not moving. There was no Rhyming Man to show him the way. He was caught in the city. No, Lew would not be caught! He could not be!

If the Rhyming Man was not there to show him the way,

could Kristie do it instead?

She tried to think herself back into the hall. But there was no chance. She still stood under the bright moon facing the dark, dead blot of a city. Both Lisa and the Rhyming Man had said no one could go back. But she must do something so Lew could come out! He did not belong in that bad place; he belonged Outside.

How had the Rhyming Man brought them out? Could Kristie somehow *think* right into Lew's mind as Lisa thought into hers? Could she let him know what to do? She would have to try.

Kristie closed her eyes so she could no longer see the dark trap of the city. She made herself imagine Lew in the hall. Yes! There he was.

Now—

Into her mind came the words of the Rhyming Man's song:

> *"See-saw, sacaradown,*
> *Now which is the way to London*
> *Town?*
> *Put one foot up, the other down.*
> *This is the way to London Town."*

Lew must—he must hear! Three times Kristie repeated the rhyme.

Lew was moving! A red square, then a yellow, a green, a blue, two squares to be covered by a hop to another red one. Yellow again, then a hop to a green block, over farther to a red.

* * *

Lew sang the words which seemed to come from nowhere into his mind. He was not sure they were the right ones. Nor could he explain how he thought of them. Somehow they seemed to be what he must say.

The first nonsense rhyme came to an end. But other words followed in the same strange way:

> "Intery, mintery, cutery corn;
> Appleseed and apple thorn;
> Wine, brier, lumber-lock.
> Five fat geese in one flock.
> Sit you now and let us sing,
> Out about and in again!"

Lew dropped down on a yellow block, not knowing what came next. So far nothing had happened, except for the fact the blocks burned brightly as he trod on them.

Out on the hillside Kristie stood statue still. Reddy had fallen unnoticed from her grasp. She cupped both hands tightly over her eyes and tried to remember what the Rhyming Man had done next. She said aloud:

> "Seeing's believing—no, no, no!
> Believing's seeing, you can go!"

It was hard for her to see Lew. Now only his face was steady in her mind.

"*Lew!*" She called his name both out loud and in her mind. "Lew! Do as I think! Please, Lew, do as I think.

> *"Now we dance, looby, looby,*
> *looby—"*

Kristie could not see if Lew was moving in the right way. There was still just his face in her mind. Did his lips move? Was he also singing the rhyme? Kristie could not be sure.

> *"Now we dance, looby, looby, looby,*
> *light."*

More nonsense words came into Lew's mind and he chanted them aloud.

> *"Look to your left hand,*
> *Now to your right!"*

Move to the left block, then back to the right. He did this twice though he had no idea what was making him. He only knew that he must. What came next?

Kristie remained still, her eyes covered. The Rhyming Man had pointed next and then they had gone. But the Rhyming Man was not there with Lew. There was no one to point. The rest—how should she do the rest when she was here and not there? A Rhyming Man to point—

She did not try to keep Lew steady in her mind now. The Rhyming Man must be there to bring Lew out—he must! She must make the Rhyming Man with a mind picture, she told herself, or Lew will stay locked Inside forever.

* * *

There was a strange flickering in the air. Lew stood watching it numbly. There was nothing in his mind now, not even more rhymes. He had a feeling he had lost something. No, he *must* believe! He must keep on believing that somehow he was going to reach Kristie, that this was the way he would find her.

The flickering steadied into a hazy figure which slowly grew more solid and brighter. The Rhyming Man! Lew shifted from one foot to the other. He sensed that this was a most important moment. He would reach Kristie now or never. And he must believe he would make it.

"Eeery, Orrey, Ickery, Ann—"

This time the song was only a ghostly whisper. The features of the Rhyming Man were not clear to Lew. He tried to see the stranger better and forced himself to believe he could.

As Lew concentrated, the Rhyming Man's face grew more distinct. The boy could make out the eyes now, and then a mouth shaping the nonsense words which must have a necessary meaning.

"Fillison, Follison, Nicholas John.
Queevy, Quavey, English Navy."

The Rhyming Man was still a little hazy. But his long arm was rising jerkily and his outstretched finger pointed straight at the boy.

"Out—goes—you!"

Lew heard the hoarse whisper. He saw the pointed finger level at his head. This was the way to Kristie! It was, he willed, it was!

There was the feeling that he was falling or flying. Lew could not tell which. He was afraid, but still he held on to the belief. This was the way to Kristie, the only way. *Believing must be seeing!*

He dropped on something softer than the pavement on which he had been standing.

"Lew!"

Opening his eyes, he saw her. He held out his arms as Kristie flung herself upon him, pushing him back against the ground. This—this was indeed Kristie. But where were they?

"Outside, Lew, we're Outside!" Her voice was joyful. She held Lew as if she would never let him go again.

Outside? Although there were no streetlamps here, there was still light. What light?

"The moon, Lew." Kristie pointed to a bright ball in the dark sky. "There are stars, too. And the Rhyming Man told me:

> 'Star light, star bright,
> First star I see tonight,
> I wish I may, I wish I might,
> Have the wish I wish tonight.'

"I wished you'd come, Lew. And you did!"

The boy shook his head as if to bring his whirling

thoughts to order. He was sure he had not said a word since he had found Kristie. Yet she knew what he was thinking. How could she?

Now she laughed. "'*Believing's seeing,*'" she repeated. "When we come Outside, we can understand what people think. It's true, Lew, it's really true!"

He felt as if his head were still in a dizzy whirl. Kristie had gotten to her feet, but she still held on to his hand. Now she tugged, pulling him up. When Lew was standing, she caught up Reddy.

Lew looked around wonderingly. Outside? But Outside was dead, poisoned. No one could live Outside.

"They can now." Again Kristie had read his thoughts. "When the people went Inside, the dead world began to change. The good came back. Look, Lew—" She pointed to something behind him.

Lew turned. There was a black, ugly blot on the land.

"That's the city, that's Inside," Kristie told him. "We can't go back—ever. But maybe the rest can come out. I'm going to try to *think* Fanna out. If you help me, Lew, maybe we can. I thought about you and got you out."

"Where—" for the first time he spoke. He had reached out and twitched a leaf from a twig on the bush beside him. It was real; he could feel it between his fingertips.

"It's all real!" Kristie agreed. "We're in London Town. That's what Lisa and the rest call it. Because of the bridge—"

"What bridge?" Lew still felt as if he were struggling in the midst of a dream.

"London Bridge. We're to build it up again. We're the stones, you see—

> *"Build it up with stone, my dears,*
> *It will stand a thousand years."*

"We just have to be careful and not do what the Olds did before. We have to keep the Outside as it is now and not try to make it like Inside. That's so ugly." Kristie made a face in the direction of the city.

"The Rhyming Man—" Lew said. "Who is the Rhyming Man and why—"

Moonlight shimmered and formed a figure. In this softer light the Old's clothing glittered again as he bowed to them.

"This time I didn't *think* you," Kristie said. "You must be real. And, you see, you were wrong—Lew did come!"

He nodded and smiled at them both.

> *"When Little's Big,*
> *The time has come*
> *For men to cast*
> *Their final sum."*

Kristie shook her head. "I don't know what that means. And I can't read what you are thinking."

Still smiling, he shook his head with the same vigor as he

had nodded. Lew watched him narrowly.

"You mean this is a second chance for us and there won't be another?"

This time the Rhyming Man nodded.

"Who are you?" Lew pressed. "And why—?"

The Rhyming Man raised his finger to his lips as if Lew were a Little who must be warned into silence.

But a thought stirred in the boy's mind. Perhaps the Rhyming Man was not a real Old after all. Perhaps long ago those in the city had hoped that Outside would be free someday. There were machines which were as strange as the blocks which answered to dancing and rhymes.

Could a machine also have the appearance of a man—say a Rhyming Man?

Only, as Lew looked into those very wise eyes watching him so keenly, he no longer cared who or what the Rhyming Man was. That he existed at all was the important thing.

The Rhyming Man gave a high hop and a very wide smile as if he approved of the direction Lew's thoughts had taken. Now he pointed down the slope to where "London Town" lay by the brook.

> "Good night.
> Sleep tight.
> Wake up bright,
> In the morning light.
> To do what's right,
> With all your might!"

He winked out as if he were a light which had been turned off.

"Come on," Kristie tugged again at Lew's hand. "We've got such a lot to do tomorrow. We must get Fanna out and the others—everyone that we can."

Lew laughed. He felt so free. This was Outside, not Inside.

"I know." He started down the slope with her. "There's London Bridge to build. Strong enough to stand for a thousand years."

MOON MIRROR

Alathi edged farther into the brush where she had left her backpack. The provisions within it she had added to during the past five days by judicious thievery while she had dogged the caravan. Now she held a last such trophy in one hand, the claw knife of her people in the other. The cape hood of her jerkin hid her silky blue-gray hair and formed a half mask covering her face near to the chin, so that in this dawn hour she was a gray-brown shadow well able to fade into the desolate countryside.

This leather wallet, which she had filched from the tent of the master trader himself, was plump, the most promising she could find. Only, since she had crept away from the camp a new uneasiness had arisen in her, leading the furlike hair on the nape of her neck to twitch. Thus she did not hurry to plunder her prize, rather sat cross-legged, running her fingers back and forth across its worn leather.

Yes, there was something. . . .

The wallet was old. She could trace only by touch a design cut into its surface. The fringe across its bottom seam protruded like the stubs of broken teeth. She fingered those.

Her hand jerked. She raised her fingers to her lips as if they had been thrust into flames and she must so lick them cool. There was also a taste—acrid, almost as if she crunched ashes.

With her knife she worried the stitches, sawing through tight strands. This seam was wider than it looked to be. What it contained had been so long hidden that she had to use knife point to loosen it from embedding leather.

A narrow thread-ribbon of metal lay as limber across her palm as if it were a chain, save that it was one piece, not linked. It was silver, untarnished, and across it played flashes of color. The two ends were thicker, one forming a loop, the other a hook, so that they might be joined.

Though Alathi had never seen its like before, her inner sense told her this was a thing of power. As a hunting cat could fix upon prey, so could her race recognize such. They told tales of these things among themselves. Perhaps those were no tales in truth, rather fragments of history of a people who had once been rulers. That day was far past. "Hill Cats" had been prey for lowland hunters for years. Still they had not lost their pride nor command of special senses. Alathi knew the worth of what she held now as if it were shouted aloud at a Fire Feast. Its touch made her flesh tingle, the skin of her whole arm roughen. Her hand closed into a fist as she shivered at her roused feelings.

Then she dared to hook it about her throat where it lay as snug as if fashioned for her alone. She pulled her jerkin higher, laced the breast thongs tight to hide it. Its purpose she had yet to learn, but she was certain now she had been guided to its hiding place.

There was no food in the wallet pouch, rather a thick wad of folded parchment. Alathi freed this. Did she hold the same map she had watched the Merchant Coultar refer to yesterday when his wains had set up camp?

The Merchant Coultar—her green-yellow eyes narrowed. Why had this man among all those who had sheltered in the inn she had spied upon drawn her interest enough that she had chosen to skulk in his wake? He was taller than most lowlanders, fair of hair and skin, where they were loweringly dark. Born of a different people she had guessed—perhaps from across the salt sea where few now voyaged since the world had been rift and burnt by the long war. He was no lordling by his dress—but his manner, that was something else. Both his own men and the guard of blankshields he had with him jumped to his word, though he never raised his voice. And see where he had boldly led them. . . .

Anatray!

Alathi hunched her shoulders, refusing to look westward. If Coultar had come seeking what stood there he was sun-touched, or ghost-ridden! She had thought to prey on these travelers long enough to get back to the hills, out of this war-riven land which had been drowned in blood so long. But she had not thought that *these* were the hills that company sought.

They made a black fringe across the sky; did he propose to win beyond their barrier, set up a trade flag for the nomads? That was folly upon folly, for there were too many blood feuds between herdsmen and coast dwellers.

No, he had made camp, a well planned one, Alathi thought critically—probably protected against any except a "Hill Cat." Still it was in short distance of that one peak ahead—that shaped by spirits for an emphatic warn-off. The spire formed an unmistakable fist, thumb curled into palm, fore and small fingers pointed skyward. Just so did prudent men gesture against ill luck and dark omens.

There were legends of the Fist, chiefly that it marked Anatray—a treasure site which might be anything from a forgotten temple to the tomb of a world ruler. Men had sought it out—there were always greedy fools. None had returned. Even those who camped nearby suffered from plague or wind-earth storms. Those who survived raved of unseen things which rode the wind.

How could Coultar have recruited men to follow him here? The wain men might be long oath-bound to his service, and the blankshields without hope of another lord, but they were all good at their jobs. She had had to exert herself these past days to keep up with them and evade their scouts.

Alathi's growing curiosity was like an itch tormenting some place she could not reach to scratch. Thus she had stayed with them past the point of prudence. Not only wanting to know where they went—but because this man Coultar teased her with a strong desire to learn more of him.

Her people continued to live only because they used well their eyes, their ears, any other inborn talent. She could prowl that camp by night, sending forth sooth-thoughts to the horses, eluding any sentry. But in all her skulking she had learned nothing of the merchant's plans.

No "Hill Cat" could trust one of another race, especially one plainsborn. Still she observed the merchant with care. He appeared to walk as softly as one of her own kind, never raising his voice (still men jumped at his bidding), his eyelids half lowered lazily, sometimes a faint half smile about his lips, as if he found in life some secret jest. He was unlike any other merchant she had observed. His power, she had decided, came not out of his purse, but was a part of him.

Now she studied the parchment, crossed by straggling lines, pricked here and there by symbols which she could not read. There was a strange odor wafting up out of its creases—as if it had lain as a covering for spices. She gnawed upon her lower lip. Perhaps her choice of the wallet had been a sorry mistake—it might be quickly missed.

As she looked from it to the land about, she found it hard to decide whether this was a representation of what she saw. Unconsciously her hand went to her throat where the band felt warm. That find had been so long hidden perhaps even Coultar had not known of it.

There was a stir in the camp. Coultar and the guard commander were mounting horses. Five of the other men also led out mounts. The girl stuffed the map back into the wallet, shoved that into her backpack, before she transformed her thin body into a misshapen outline by shrugging on the pack itself.

The horsemen trotted out, heading for the Fist. Alathi watched for a moment. If she did have Coultar's map, he had not missed it. However, he seemed entirely confident of his way. If she were wise she would stay where she was. However, that itch of curiosity would not allow her that safety.

She eyed every possible cover before her, knowing she must let them get well ahead before she followed. Last night they had unloaded some of the boxes in the wains, moving them with such ease as to suggest those were empty. If Coultar had not carried goods—then he was prepared to find such here. The fabled treasure of Anatray?

Alathi was returning to the home hills with nothing. Her people had been harried for years by the lowlanders. Suppose she let this merchant take the risk of looting the unknown and then help herself, as she was confident she was able to do, from what he garnered? She had nothing left save her skill and perhaps—again her fingers sought that throat band—that was not so poor a heritage that she would not profit.

She could not push from her mind the fantasy that, in some manner, she was linked with Coultar; that his good fortune might be turned to her use also. Every time she watched the man she had felt the harnessed power in him, recognized that he was one who would be master not servant in fortune's train.

So what if he rode now into demon-haunted land? After all, death had brushed her times without number during the past years. She must have long ago used up the number of "lives" which had been sung at her birthing. If she were to die, what would it matter? She was alone, and that stark loneliness strode always at her side, set upon her a weariness beyond the power of banishing. It slept with her, matched steps, haunted the night hours when she could not sleep.

Alathi flung up her head, the pride of her people rising hot in her. Legends sometimes possessed a core of truth. If there was aught ahead for the bold to seize she would take it. If it was for ill . . . that she was well accustomed to.

Sure that the goal of the riders was the Fist, Alathi made flitting rushes from one bit of cover to the next, watching the men rather than the demon spire. She had patience, freezing into the land whenever one of them looked about.

Now she struck north, away from their track, intending to come down from a different direction. The party had reached the Fist, three men remaining with the mounts, the rest, with Coultar, disappearing around its base.

Alathi lay belly down behind an outcrop of rock. The horse guards were alert, crossbows to hand. They were patroling, but they made no attempt to go beyond the Fist. She still had a chance to retreat, but she also knew that she would never take it.

There was a promising line of shadow along the foot of the

hills. She headed for that. Her breast heaving, she crouched low, waiting to hear a shout, even the whistle of a dart. No sound. Heartened, she scuttled on.

The ridge she followed broke; here was a cut which might hold a roadway. She sped ahead and now the Fist itself was between her and the guards. A pavement, but of a different stone than that which formed the bones of this land, had been set by purpose to form a path into the hills. It led through a dark canyon, along the shadowed throat where Coultar and his men already moved.

Their pace was slow, as suited those scouting the unknown, the men glancing from side to side, bare steel or crossbows ready. Yet Coultar marched as one who knew where he would go, looking only at something which he cupped in the palm of his hand, an object too small to be a map.

Alathi sidled along the wall of that half-hidden road. So intent was she upon following undetected, she had no preparation for what came. Her head jerked forward with such force she toppled to her knees, her hand clawing at her throat where that band had tightened, setting her gasping for air, black fear blotting out the world—everything except the need to loosen that choking thread of metal.

She tore with frantic fingers at the constriction, striving to slide the hook from the loop. Then she felt an urgency—a need. Only it was not *her* need—not now—for the loop loosened of itself, as if its sharp attack had come only to establish control over her, as if some presence that could reach her neither by voice nor gesture so claimed her full attention.

Gasping, rubbing her neck, she was filled with a new fear; she could not understand from whence this power came or what use it sought to make of her.

Blackness walled her. Yet she feebly struggled against the void that would use her for its own purpose. She was blind, voiceless, still she held desperately to an inner core of self, stubborn even in the face of what might be death.

Only dimly did she sense that she had regained her feet, was lurching from side to side as she ran, that something within urged her to ever greater effort, blotting out caution. She mouthed words which she heard, though they arose from no thought or will of her own:

"Ye Lords of the Four Watchtowers, ye are called upon. Rise to bear witness, arm to guard! The Great One who comes is the beauty and the bounty of the green earth. Her crown is the white moon among the spinning stars. From Her all things proceed, and have proceeded, from the birth of the world. To Her all things, in due time, return. She is the beginning and the ending. In Her hands lie strength, power, compassion, honor, humility, mirth and awe.

"Those who seek Her shall do so in vain if they know not the mysteries, nor call upon Her with the names of power. If they do not find such knowledge within, then it shall be closed to them without.

"Blessed are the eyes which can indeed behold Her in Her glory, mark Her path to follow. Blessed is the mouth which sings Her praise. Blessed be the body which is fruitful in Her service, blessed the feet walking in Her ways.

"Her names are many among the living, thus those who do Her honor call upon Her in diverse ways. She is Isis, and Astarte, Bast, Curwen, Diana, Skula, Freya, Ya-ling, Britta. . . .

"Blessed be!"

The blindness had lifted, she could clearly see the men ahead. As one they had turned to stare. One of the crossbows raised, a dart lay ready to fire. Still she could only run helplessly on.

Coultar's hand swung out, knocked down that bow. He strode forward, as if to meet her, his eyes now wide open, a strange look on his face. He might be seeing the very treasure that he had come seeking. But it was not the merchant she must meet—no. The force that drew her lay beyond—the Inner Place which belonged to *Her,* the Shining One!

Helplessly possessed, Alathi prepared to dodge, running more swiftly and surely, while that within assured greater control of her body. She was now only a tool—or a weapon—for another's use!

As she passed Coultar, avoiding his grasp, she saw his face fully alive. He had dropped some mask which had shielded him. There was avid eagerness in his wide eyes, his lips parted hungrily. He flung up his hand in the hollow of which rested a silvery disc. From that burst a thin flash of light.

Alathi pawed at the neck of her jerkin. The band about her throat was heating again. Words once more came to her even as she passed him by:

"*She* is the Great One whom no *man* dares name, though Her names are as many as there are nations, clans, and kin. She holds life in one hand, in the other the sword of death, maintaining the balance of the world. She welcomes the fall of seed into the waiting furrow, the growth that arises from the seed, the reaping of it when it ripens. She faces, unfearing, the coming of cold and of the winter sleep. For this is the pattern—"

One of the men against the wall put out his hand swiftly, then shrank back. Perhaps the force that dwelt in her now had shown itself in some way—perhaps even Coultar had signed some order. Alathi slid between them as if they were not there.

More words spilled from her jerkily as she ran. These were different, clicking, guttural, so unlike her own speech that the very sound terrified her. She could not stop uttering them—they seemed to arise from a mind portion where not even memory still lay.

Before her now was only the narrowing ancient road, down which she must go, helplessly. Nor did she fall into silence, for she singsonged, croaked, sometimes repeated phrases which made some sense, until her mouth dried and her throat ached. Nor could she rest while that inner one remained in command.

The walls, formed by the heights, drew together; now she was in a tunnel, a dark way. At its entrance had shimmered a haze curtain across which colors crossed, even as such had swept across the neckband's silver surface.

"Lord of the Watch Tower of the West—" She was once more speaking sense. "I am summoned. Speed you my way, for to this summoning there must be no hindrance—"

Through the haze she burst, feeling a flash of intense cold, as if she had broken a skim of ice across a winter prisoned pond. The way was no longer dark, the haze encased her.

Now the fear which had struck at the beginning of this wild and unaccountable action ebbed, not to rise again. In its place welled excitement akin to that she had felt days earlier when she had first seen Coultar.

"By the Lady. . . ." Those words she had willed herself. "By the favor of the Lady. . . ."

The haze swirled faster about her, its colors like jewels whirled about on cords—blazing into fantastic brilliance. She came forth from the tunnel.

Abruptly whatever had driven her withdrew, even as a man might snap his fingers. Alathi swayed, now aware of a sharp pain in her side, her aching feet, the dryness of her mouth. But those were of the body—they meant little or nothing in this place.

Here were no rocks, no earth. Rather there lay a mirror of silver water in a round basin filling all the space between straight cliffs, those as smooth as if they had been deliberately chiseled so that none might find footing upon them. Across the mirror once more played those flashes of vivid color, rippling as might the waves of the salt sea.

The surface of the pool (or lake, for it extended for a far distance) was opaque. One could not see below. Around it ran a curbing near as tall as her waist. She staggered toward that, energy seeping out of her, not only weak and trembling, but bereft, as one whose treasure has been snatched by an enemy.

She fell to her knees behind the curbing, her hand steadying her. As Alathi clung there, near to the edge of consciousness, she saw the other wonder of this stretch of water. The sun shone down, well on its westward journey. Only the brilliance of that was not mirrored below.

Rather there rested on the surface a disc, growing outward from the heart of the lake. No shadow broke the pale, perfect round. Still there appeared upon it certain changes of color. Alathi, marking those, first dully and then with awakening recognition, knew what it resembled. Just as the moon was so clouded here and there so did the same patterns appear.

She wailed, voicing the low, keening cry uttered by the women of her own people as they leapt and danced beneath silver rays in the ancient rites of their sex. Alathi's body twitched as if she would dance—as if—

She pulled herself up, shrugged off her backpack, not caring where it might fall. From her thigh sheath she drew her long sword knife; from her belt her "claw"—such must not be worn here.

Straight she stood, watching that disc on the water grow ever more distinct, as if it were solid. Deep in her throat Alathi voiced a sound which was very old, reaching back into the first beginnings of her people, beginnings which even legends could not touch. She took a high step, to balance on the top of the curb, her eyes only for the moon shape.

Then—

Pain!

So sharp that it split through her skull like the blade of an axe. She wailed, writhed, fell back into a darkness which she thought fleetingly was death. No fear—just loss, a loss which was also pain—then nothing at all.

Distant sounds broke through the envelope of the dark. She strove to hold the dark intact. It promised safety and rest from troubling. Flashes of memory followed, too fleeting to be held.

"—Hill Cat! Best cut her throat, lord. They're as treacherous as a bal-serpent and nearly as deadly. Do they not dance evil down from the moon and spread it abroad in the dark of night?"

"Stand away! This one has in her what I have long sought. If you fear, Damstiff, then back with you. She is indeed a holder of power past your guessing!"

Alathi felt the band of fire about her throat. Only it did not burn, rather from it she drew strength, urging her out of the safety she had sought in the dark. She was aware of her body though she did not yet open her eyes, lay limp in another's hold.

Those voices used the hated click-click of lowland speech. Fragments wheeled through her mind in broken pictures. She could not hold onto them long enough to gain meaning—

"Ahhhhh!"

A scream rang in her ears, pierced through her head. She had been lifted, was being carried—No! The pool—they would take her from the pool!

The clash of steel, a smell . . . she had scented that before. The map . . . an old map and from its creases this same spicy odor. He who held her was moving. Did she have a chance to wriggle free? A second scream choked off in the midpoint as if a throat could no longer give it passage.

Alathi opened her eyes and, at the same moment, made her bid for freedom, twisting her body sharply. Coultar held her, but his head was half turned away as if his attention were drawn elsewhere. She was free of his hold, tumbling, to bring up, back against an earth wall—in the tunnel.

One of the guardsmen staggered by her, his hands to his face, weaving from side to side as if blind. Another, his mouth twisted by fear, leaned against the wall opposite her, seeking to aim, in spite of trembling hands, his crossbow. Then he screamed, a high cry like a woman's, hurled the weapon from him. Out of it, as it crashed on the pavement, curled a feather of pale smoke, then white flames leaped.

He whose weapon that was screamed again, pulled himself away from the wall, still staring at the crossbow, his features a mask of terror passing the bounds of sanity.

Alathi looked to Coultar. He held no steel—perhaps he had dropped weapons when he had taken her captive. Swinging nearly completely around, his face that of a sentry alert to attack, he looked back to the pool. Both of his hands were now heart high, and in the right one was that disc.

Those with him had all fled. Knowing that she had nothing now to fear from them the girl straightened. Strength came flowing back. She willed it to her as she might at the end of a training bout. Her breath no longer came in ragged gasps, rather smoothly as a precious draught of water in the desert. With herself once more under control she became more and more aware of a force which filled this narrow way. It was so strong that she believed she might put forth a hand and gather up its substance.

It was not aimed at her. Coultar's face grew more tense, he began to breathe faster. His lips were forced back against his teeth in a half snarl of effort as he visibly fought for speech:

"By Curwen, by Thethera, by Skula, by the oak, the ash, the red thorn, by the waxing moon—the moon that is full—that which wanes. By—"

He passed into another language, one in which the sound began low in his throat, ascending note by note to a higher pitch than she could believe any man might naturally utter.

The disc he held was no longer that. Rather he cupped length of white flame. His fingers writhed, blistered before her eyes, still he held it, and stood, rock firm.

"By the Law of the Worlds, and that which lies between them, by those who walk still our paths, and those who have gone before," he dropped into intelligible speech again. "In the name of Herne, Thoth, Abyis, Lord of Light, by Suth, and Korn, also the Watch Lords of the East, West, North, and South, do I stand here. Two things that have contact—" he held the flame a fraction higher—"will come together. A power strengthens a power. O, *She* who—"

The flame in his hand leaped free. To Alathi it sped. He wheeled to face the girl as that flame struck against the latched hoop at her throat, clung, changed. She felt no fire, from the uniting came no harm to her.

Alathi raised hands to the disc once more formed, then she

tretched out the right slowly to the man who had held it arlier. A wall might have fallen—she saw. He was no merchant—rather a seeker—one who was a stranger, still loser than any kin.

She gasped, for his body seemed to flow, to change. This was ot the man she had followed secretly across the waste of Ghritz. Though something of that one remained. Only more ad been revealed.

"Who are you!" she asked.

"There is the Lady." There was a weight in his words as if he were one of more authority than she had ever met. "There is also He who comes with the winter—into whose hands *She* asses the Sword, that He may complete that circle which balances the world—Life and birth, death and sleep, before life omes anew. I am one who is vowed to that Lord of Winter. He as been lost from the time and people of my birth world; thus must journey into another time and place to call upon him gain for the sake of my own kind.

"Evoe, Evoe, Pan! Evoe, Herne! Evoe, Thoth!" He threw ack his head. His voice came as a great shout which seemed to ock the very world under and about them.

Again he changed. Here stood a dark-skinned man who wore the spotted skin of some beast about him over a white ilt; another with a head of close-curled hair, his body bare ave for a small strip of hide, the badge of kinship with the world of beasts; a man in armor; one in a long robe across hich ran runes in scarlet, to glow and fade. He was all these, et also the Coultar of the here and now.

"I swear by the wide and fruitful womb of my mother, by my honor among men, by the blood shed in the Circle—" He spoke softly, as if he sought some answer from her. Though her ears still rang from his shouts, she could hear.

Alathi answered, knowing, even as she spoke, that she had said the words before many times. When and in what places? That did not matter now—this was the time, the place, to which she had been led so that she might say them again and so enter into what waited.

"I swear by my hope of the Great Glory beyond, by my past lives, my hope of future ones yet to come—"

At last their hands might meet. Around them surged the power. Not driven by it, but a part of it, they went back—Hill Cat and merchant no longer. What they were now they must learn.

They came out to the pool. Alathi understood. In each life there waits a door to the Innerworld ready. Some never found it. That she had was as fair a fortune as the stuff of dreams.

"Blessed Lady, I am thy child—"

"—thy child," he echoed her.

Together they climbed upon the curbing; together the leaped, hand in hand, out into the great waiting moon mirror. closed about them, drew them in. However, their search ha only begun, their feet but touched upon the first steps of th widest and straightest road of all.